SPACE JACKERS

THE PIRATE KING

HUW POWELL

BLOOMSBURY

LONDON OXFORD NEW YORK NEW DELHI SYDNEY

Bloomsbury Publishing, London, Oxford, New York, New Delhi and Sydney

First published in Great Britain in January 2017 by Bloomsbury Publishing Plc
50 Bedford Square, London WC1B 3DP

www.bloomsbury.com

BLOOMSBURY is a registered trademark of Bloomsbury Publishing Plc

A CIP catalogue record for this book is available from the British Library

ISBN 978 1 4088 4766 4

Typeset by Integra Software Services Pvt. Ltd.
Printed and bound in Great Britain by CPI Group (UK) Ltd, Croydon CR0 4YY

1 3 5 7 9 10 8 6 4 2

For my wife, Beata

Prologue

A Cold Day on Shan-Ti

Snow was falling outside and galactic war seemed inevitable.

Kristina Lemark sat alone in the prime minister's office on Shan-Ti, an independent colony at the heart of the fourth solar system. The walls surrounding her were lined with portraits of former leaders, while in her hands she clutched a framed photograph of the prime minister's family. It was hard to believe that he was gone and she was now in charge of the planet.

The prime minister had died the previous day, when a political gathering on nearby Santanova had ended in a shocking explosion, killing all of the independent colony leaders. A display screen in the corner of the office replayed horrific scenes of devastation, which had been broadcast by the *Interstellar News* moments before the stellar-net signal was lost. These images were mixed with extracts of a speech by a teenage space pirate called Jake Cutler, who had claimed to be the ruler of a mythical planet, Altus.

Kristina snorted mirthlessly. 'What kind of parents raise their child to be a spacejacker?'

Before the explosion, Jake had told the gathering of leaders that the Interstellar Government was planning to wipe out the independent colonies. He'd claimed that despite centuries of peace, the Interstellar Government now wanted to extend its control beyond the United Worlds and take over the entire galaxy. Incredibly, the leaders had not only accepted this story, they had even signed a treaty to unite the independent colonies, before the explosion took their lives.

Was the boy really from Altus? If there were a planet with three crystal moons and gold dust-desert, surely the Galactic Trade Corporation would have sniffed it out by now. After all, those corporate crooks were the number one crystal supplier in the galaxy. Kristina detested the power of crystals. Shan-Ti had its own currency, the same as the other independent colonies, but crystals were accepted everywhere, which made them extremely valuable. A lot of good people had been corrupted by crystal greed.

There was still no stellar-net signal that morning, which meant that Shan-Ti was unable to communicate with other independent colonies, or anyone else for that matter. The local news had reported rumours of fighting in the seventh solar system, but there was no way to check if these were true. Did this mean that Jake Cutler was telling the truth?

Kristina doubted that the Interstellar Navy had enough warships to attack all of the independent colonies. But then again, the Interstellar Government had just signed a treaty with the alien Gorks to form a new fleet. Had the Gorks been hired to do the dirty work? Kristina disliked those vile, brutish creatures, with their vacant black eyes, rubbery blue skin and stubby head fins. How long would it be before one of their warships attacked Shan-Ti?

With a shiver, she put down the photograph and checked the time. In a matter of minutes, the Shan-Ti war council would resume, so they could decide how best to defend their planet. Kristina dreaded the prospect of facing more questions. There were already people camped outside the building, pointing fingers and demanding answers.

What happened on Santanova?

Why is there no stellar-net?

What is the deputy prime minister doing about it?

Kristina had no answers to these questions, but she was determined to be strong. At least, until her people could elect a new leader. Before he had left for the gathering, the prime minister had asked her to look after Shan-Ti; therefore she was going to do everything in her power to honour his wish.

As she sat there, a colourful four-winged bird swooped past the frosted window, battling its way through the dense blizzard outside. It had been decades since snow had settled on Shan-Ti and Kristina was glad to be inside the warm office. The colonists had taken their hot climate for granted and few of them knew how to cope in the cold. Would they blame her for the weather as well?

With that thought, she brushed a curtain of blonde hair away from her face and activated the intercom.

'Charlie, you had better order a stack of stellar-burgers and a bucket of fried vegetables. It's going to be a long one.'

'Yes, ma'am,' responded the assistant. 'The war council is due to start in two minutes. There's fresh coffee in the room and I've told the local news that they will have to wait for a statement.'

'Thank you,' she said. 'Has there been any word from the other colonies?'

'Not yet, but Father Benedict is here to see you.'

'The cyber-abbot?' Kristina massaged her tired eyes with the palms of her hands. 'This is not the time to talk about technology.'

'I told him that you were busy, but he insists on seeing you.' Charlie lowered his voice. 'He says that he has information about Jake Cutler.'

Kristina considered this for a moment.

'OK, send him in,' she said. 'And tell the war council that I'm running late.'

'Yes, ma'am.'

Kristina sat back in her executive chair as Father Benedict entered the office. His face was flushed and his bald head glowed pink in a nest of white hair. It was rare for him to leave the monastery where his cyber-monks studied and worshipped technology.

'Good day, deputy prime minister,' said the cyber-abbot, brushing the snow from his thick black robes.

'Welcome, father. I understand that you have some information for me?'

Father Benedict closed the door. 'It's about the boy ruler, Jake Cutler. He was here, on Shan-Ti, less than a week before the gathering on Santanova.'

'Here?'

'Yes, his crew stayed in the crater outside the monastery for a few days to repair their ship. I was with him when he discovered the plot to wipe out the independent colonies.' Father Benedict pulled up a seat. 'Jake was telling the truth about the United

Worlds. It was their Interstellar Government that blew up our leaders.'

'How can you be so sure?' she asked. 'The Cutler boy was last seen running from the gathering. For all we know, he caused the explosion. What's the saying? Never trust a space pirate.'

Father Benedict shook his head. 'The Interstellar Government wants to start a galactic war. My cyber-monks have been using our satellites to hack their naval communications.'

'You've been spying?'

'I would prefer to call it information gathering. The word on the stars is that the war has already started in the seventh solar system. It won't be long before the fighting spreads and more independent colonies are attacked, until the Interstellar Government controls the entire galaxy.'

Kristina's sharp features hardened. 'Why are they doing this?'

Father Benedict stroked his neat white beard. 'From what we can gather, the crystal shortage is worse than people realise. If prices keep rising, the galaxy will be facing another mega-depression. But if the independent colonies are turned into United Worlds, the Interstellar Government can rip them apart in search of more crystals. The Galactic Trade

Corporation will be allowed to mine wherever it wants, as long as it splits the profits with the Interstellar Government, of course.'

Kristina's face soured. 'Are you telling me that millions of people will die over crystals? We have to stop this madness.'

'Yes, but how?' Father Benedict creased his brow. 'All of the leaders are dead, and without the stellar-net, there's no way to contact the other independent colonies. In fact, we cannot even appeal to the Interstellar Government on their capital planet, Domus. I'm afraid that Shan-Ti must prepare for the worst.'

'What are you saying?'

'No one can help us. We're on our own.'

Chapter 1

Refugees

Jake Cutler woke with a start. It took him a moment to remember where he was and why he was dressed in his Altian uniform. The leather chair rubbed noisily as he sat up and glanced around the bridge of the *Star Chaser*, where Captain Swan and several shipmates were operating the luxurious spacecraft in silence. Jake was not part of the crew. He was merely a passenger who hadn't paid his way. How long had he been asleep?

In his drowsy state, Jake tried to convince himself that the gathering on Santanova had been a dream, but as the blanket slipped from his lap, he noticed several cuts on his hands, which were proof of his narrow escape. It was hard to believe that all of the independent colony leaders were gone. All, except him. How ironic that the only leader to escape from Santanova was the thirteen-year-old ruler of a planet that wasn't supposed to exist. Except, Altus was real. It had remained hidden for centuries inside the Tego Nebula dust cloud, before Jake and his friends had discovered it.

There was no proof that the Interstellar Government had planted a mega-bomb on Santanova, but who else wanted the leaders out of the way? With one explosion, the Interstellar Government was now free to wage war on the independent colonies. At that very moment, Jake knew the Interstellar Navy was surrounding colonies in the seventh solar system, including Remota, where he had been raised. Vantos was already under attack and who knew how many other planets were fighting off naval warships.

Jake had to find a way to contact the independent colonies, before it was too late. No single planet was strong enough to resist on its own, but together they might stand a chance. He was the only leader to survive the explosion on Santanova, therefore it was up to him to lead the colonies to war, united. In his heart, he knew that it was the right thing to do, yet the thought of it terrified him. The explosion had shaken him more than he cared to admit. It had made him realise how fragile life was and just how easily it could be extinguished.

Jake wished that he could return to Remota, where things had been simple. He would give anything to be back in the space docks, sketching ships and drinking apple juice. But his old life was gone. With a sigh, he turned his attention to a cluster of vessels on a nearby holographic display. The *Star Chaser* was leading a convoy of twelve passenger ships across the fourth solar system, each of them crammed with refugees and escorted by a handful of fighter craft. Had it only been a day since they had fled Santanova?

Kella entered the bridge and tucked a strand of black hair behind her ear. Jake had never seen his friend look so tired. Her emerald green eyes were dark and bloodshot.

'How's our lilac-skinned shipmate?' he asked, referring to their other friend, Nanoo, a Novu alien from another galaxy.

'He's much better,' she said, taking a seat. 'At least he was only shot in the arm. I've left him snoring on one of the medical bay beds. I wish that I could close my eyes without thinking about, you know, the people who died.'

There was an awkward pause as they both stared at the holographic display. A giant dust cloud formed in Jake's mind and a chorus of screams echoed in his ears.

'Mega-bombs should be banned,' he muttered. 'Just the thought of it makes me feel sick. But you need to get some rest. We can't have our best medic collapsing.'

11

Kella gave him a half-hearted nod. 'Any sign of the Interstellar Navy on the scanners?'

'Nothing yet, but we still have a long way to go and I would bet the moons of Altus that they're searching for us.'

The convoy was heading to Shan-Ti monastery, which was located in the same solar system as Santanova. Jake wanted somewhere safe to drop off the refugees. There was no way to warn the monastery that they were coming, but Jake had spent most of his life with cyber-monks and he was confident that they would help.

'Have you worked out how to contact the other colonies?' asked Kella.

'No,' said Jake. 'We could send messenger ships, but that would take too long. What we need is our own personal stellar-net, so we can send out a secret message.'

Kella rubbed her neck. 'Well, we've got to think of something fast. Vantos needs help now and we can't fight a war on our own. Have you considered asking the Interstellar Government for a ceasefire?'

'Why would they listen to me? I'm Kid Cutler, the most wanted spacejacker in the seven solar systems. We both became outlaws the moment we joined the Space Dogs crew, but it's me they're blaming for destroying the *ISS Colossus*.'

'That wasn't your fault,' she said. 'How can anyone believe that a rusty old cargo hauler like the *Dark Horse* could defeat the most advanced warship in the Interstellar Navy? We can explain that the *ISS Colossus* was claimed by a black hole.'

'And you think they'll take our word for it? The Interstellar Government knows that Admiral Nex was searching for me when the *ISS Colossus* disappeared.'

'OK, so what are we going to do?'

'There's not much we can do,' he sighed. 'Not while we're stuck aboard this ship. Let's get the refugees to Shan-Ti and then we'll work out how to save the independent colonies.'

'Has there been any word from the Space Dogs?'

'Nope. Nor anyone else for that matter. I spoke with Captain Swan earlier and he has never known the big black to be so quiet. It's as though we're the only ships left in the galaxy.'

'I expect that most crews are afraid of being attacked,' she said. 'No one knows who to trust any more.'

Jake had something else on his mind. 'I've been thinking about my dad. What if he's on Vantos, or another independent colony in the seventh solar system? He might get caught in the fighting.'

Jake's father, Andras Cutler, had been missing for eleven years, since he drifted into an asteroid field wearing a spacesuit. Most people assumed that Andras was dead, lost to the stars, but Jake had grown up believing that his father was still alive.

'We don't know anything for sure,' said Kella.

'But when I met with Jorge Dasch on Santanova, he told me that he'd seen my dad alive within the last few months, in a service port in the seventh solar system, wearing something called head-cuffs.'

'Jorge Dasch was a traitor,' she pointed out. 'How can you trust a word that man said? He sabotaged your father's ship and he tried to sell you to the Interstellar Navy.'

'But what if he was telling the truth?' groaned Jake. 'What if these head-cuffs mean that my dad is some sort of prisoner? He would be trapped when the Interstellar Navy attacked.'

'We've got to assume that he's safe. I can't bear the thought of my sister Jeyne being locked up, but I have to believe that she's OK until I find a way to rescue her.' Kella took a deep breath. 'And yes, that means taking down the Interstellar Government to save her.'

Before she became a space pirate, Kella was a United Worlds citizen. Her older sister, Jeyne, had been arrested for crimes of treason, earning her a cell in Ur-Hal, a maximum security prison planet in the first solar system. To make matters worse, the Galactic Trade Corporation now controlled their family crystal mine.

'But what if we fail?' asked Jake.

'That,' said Kella, 'is not an option.'

'My lord,' interrupted Captain Swan.

Jake looked up at the tall captain of the *Star Chaser*. Beneath his trimmed grey beard, his face was etched with concern.

'What is it?' asked Jake.

'There's a ship approaching,' said the captain.

'Is it the Interstellar Navy?'

'No, it's space pirates.'

Jake felt a leap of excitement. Had the Space Dogs found them? He had missed that crew more than he thought possible and he longed to see their old cargo hauler, the *Dark Horse*, again. But what if it wasn't them? What if it was another pirate crew? What if it was the infamous Captain James Hawker and his bloodthirsty Starbucklers? The convoy could not risk being spacejacked while it carried so many refugees.

'We can't outrun them,' said Captain Swan. 'The passenger ships are too slow. However, we do have some fighter craft and a few of the larger vessels bear laser cannon. What are your orders, my lord?'

'Hold fire until we know if they're friendly.'

Captain Swan seemed surprised. 'Forgive me, but there's no such thing as a friendly pirate. I've been spacejacked enough times to know.'

'I'm a space pirate,' said Jake. 'We're not all the same. Let me take a look.'

Captain Swan tapped the nearest display and a holographic image appeared of the approaching vessel. It was an ugly ship that looked as though it had been built by faulty robots. Jake could make out a flaming skull and crossbones on its jagged red hull. Where had he seen that emblem before?

'Well?' asked Captain Swan. 'Do you recognise it?'

Jake hesitated. 'Yes, but it can't be *that* ship, can it?'

'Which ship?'

Jake shook his head in disbelief. 'The *Black Death*.'

The words hung in the air like a sharp frost.

'But that's impossible,' said Kella. 'We blew up the *Black Death* four days ago.'

'You defeated Scarabus Shark?' exclaimed Captain Swan.

'Yes, Jake fired the laser bolt that finished him off, so there's no way that this is the same ship.' Kella peered at the display. 'It doesn't even look like the *Black Death*.'

This wasn't strictly true. The approaching vessel was smaller than the old warship, but there were definitely some similarities. It was as though someone had tried to build a miniature version of the famous pirate ship.

Jake noticed that its scorched hull was coated in a red substance. Was that blood?

'Perhaps some of the crew survived,' he said. 'And they built another ship out of the wreckage.'

'Captain,' interrupted the first mate. 'The scanners have identified the vessel. I've double-checked the registration plates and it is the *Black Death*.'

Jake wondered if he was still dreaming. How was this possible?

'If that's Scarabus Shark, this is going to get rough,' said Captain Swan. 'I want this ship ready to fire the moment we're in range.'

'Aye, captain.'

Red lights flashed on the bridge and a siren sounded. Captain Swan took one last look at the holographic display and withdrew to a control panel on the rear wall. He activated the communicator and cleared his throat.

'Attention all ships, this is Captain Swan of the *Star Chaser*. We have incoming space pirates. I want everyone on battle stations and ready to repel intruders.'

Jake heard the distant rumble of a laser cannon being rolled out of its gun port.

'What can I do to help?' he asked. 'I know how to fire a laser cannon and I've had battle experience.'

'You should remain here, on the bridge, my lord.'

'But –'

'Your bravery is admirable,' said Captain Swan. 'However, we already have an experienced gunner. I recruited her myself from the Reus planetary guard.'

'There must be something I can do,' insisted Jake. 'It doesn't feel right to wait here and do nothing, while everyone else is preparing to fight.'

'We cannot risk you getting hurt,' said the captain, firmly. 'You're too important. Who else can lead the independent colonies to war? Without you, there's no hope for any of us, including our families and home planets.'

'He's right,' said Kella. 'You'll have to sit this one out.'

The *Black Death* was a lot closer now and Jake could make out its name painted on the hull. He kept his eyes fixed on the display, trying to think of a way to help the convoy.

'Captain, we're coming into range,' reported the first mate. 'It's now or never.'

The captain nodded and activated the communicator.

'Attention all ships,' he said. 'This is Captain Swan, prepare to fire on my order.'

Chapter 2

Sanctuary

'Wait!' cried Jake. 'That's not the *Black Death*.'

'But the registration plates?' said Captain Swan.

'The ship is a fake.' Jake pointed at the display. 'It's wearing a disguise.'

Kella frowned. 'How do you know?'

Jake grinned. 'Because none of its laser cannon are moving except for one, and it's pink.'

Kella gasped.

'What does that mean?' asked Captain Swan. 'Is it a friend or foe?'

'Underneath those hull plates is a ship called the *Divine Wind*,' said Jake. 'Its captain is a teenage space pirate called Crazy Kay Jagger and she is definitely a friend.'

Kay and her crew, the Luna Ticks, had saved Jake and the Space Dogs on more than one occasion. Their old star frigate was the only ship that Jake had ever seen with pink laser cannon.

'All ships stand down,' said Captain Swan. 'Do not open fire on the approaching vessel. I repeat, do not open fire.'

Jake checked the windows and not a single laser bolt pierced the darkness. The fighter craft remained in place, positioned between the convoy and the pirate ship.

'We're being hailed,' said the first mate.

The captain adjusted his communicator. 'Ahoy, pirate ship, this is Captain Dan Swan of the *Star Chaser*. Identify yourself.'

Jake's heart drummed as he waited for the response. In his mind, he pictured Kay's freckled white face, her sapphire blue eyes and her flowing pink hair. Had he guessed right?

'Ahoy-hoy, mates,' called out a husky female voice. 'This is Captain Kay Jagger of the *Divine Wind*. I know we look like a floating shipwreck, but it's only a temporary patch job until we fix our ruptured hull. In case you're wondering, we're not the *Black Death* and we're not looking for trouble.'

'What do you want?' asked Captain Swan.

'We spotted your convoy fleeing from Santanova,' she said. 'You're heading straight for three naval warships and you need to change course immediately.'

'Why do you care what happens to us?' Captain Swan signalled to his crew to check the long-range scanners.

'I have my reasons,' she said. 'Let's just say that war is breaking out and I'm cheering for the independent colonies.'

The first mate looked up from his scanner and raised three fingers, confirming the number of naval warships.

'Thanks for the warning,' said Captain Swan. 'We're heading to planet Shan-Ti. If you really want to help the independent colonies, perhaps you should come with us.'

'What did you say?' she spluttered. 'Why would you chumpties want to travel with space pirates? Don't you know that we can't be trusted?'

The captain offered the communicator to Jake, who took it and grinned.

'I trust you, Crazy Kay Jagger.'

'Jake?'

'Hello Kay.'

'Jake Cutler? I thought you were dead. How the guff did you survive? The whole city was destroyed.'

'It's a long story, but I was in the space docks when it happened.'

'Oh,' she said, with a hint of disappointment. 'I was going to avenge your death. Are you sure you're OK? No serious injuries that need avenging?'

Jake laughed. 'I'm fine, but thanks for the offer. Kella and Nanoo are with me. We thought that your ship was the *Black Death*. Is there any chance Scarabus Shark survived?'

'Nope,' she said. 'We discovered his body when we were searching the wreckage for parts. That grumpy space jerk is nothing but kalmar bait now.'

'Where are the others?' asked Jake.

'You mean the Space Dogs?'

'Yes, did you get separated when you escaped from the Interstellar Navy?'

'In a manner of speaking,' she said gingerly.

Jake could tell that Kay was struggling to find the right words. A sense of dread stirred inside him.

'What is it?' he asked. 'What happened?'

'After you left, we had some engine trouble and the *Divine Wind* was as good as finished. I was about to give the order to abandon ship when the *Dark Horse* led away the naval warships.'

'Magnifty,' said Jake. 'And then what happened?'

'We fixed our engine and patched up our hull, but it was too late to save the *Dark Horse*.'

'Too late? What are you saying?'

'The Space Dogs have been arrested. Admiral Vantard is holding them prisoner aboard the *ISS Magnificent*.'

'What?'

'We have to help them,' said Kella.

'And they call me crazy?' laughed Kay. 'Do you really think that you can take on a naval warship with a handful of fighters and some passenger ships?'

'No,' admitted Jake. 'But who knows what Admiral Vantard is doing to the Space Dogs. Would they abandon us, if it were the other way around?'

'Aye, probably,' she said. 'Unless there was something in it for them.'

Captain Swan cleared his throat. 'I hate to interrupt, but we're wasting time, my lord. We need to leave now before the Interstellar Navy arrives.'

Jake checked the nearest display screen. What if one of those warships was the *ISS Magnificent*? It felt wrong to run away when the Space Dogs could be so near. But if they stayed, the convoy would be arrested or blown to stardust. As much as Jake wanted to help his old crew, he had hundreds of passengers to consider; the cabins and corridors of every ship were packed with innocent refugees who were relying on him to lead them to safety. He knew that their best chance was to head straight for Shan-Ti.

Jake closed his eyes and gave the order. 'Let's give those naval warships a wide berth. Set course for Shan-Ti, full speed ahead.'

When the convoy finally reached Shan-Ti, the *Star Chaser* was the first ship to enter its frosty atmosphere. The pleasure cruiser set down in the giant snow-filled crater by the cyber-monk monastery, away from the towns and settlements.

Jake found it strange to think that he had left the same spot only two weeks ago aboard the *Dark Horse*. He glanced out of the window at the monastery carved into the crater wall. Its scattered windows were sheltered beneath a cluster of huge satellite dishes, which Jake had used to contact the mayor of Remota and arrange the gathering of leaders. Nanoo had then used his advanced alien technology to boost the signal, so he could send a message to his distant home planet, Taan-Centaur.

'That's it,' said Jake. 'That's how we're going to contact the independent colonies without the stellar-net.'

Kella peered out of the window. 'The satellite dishes?'

Jake smiled and nodded.

Nanoo entered the bridge, exercising his wounded arm by swinging it in wide circles. 'What up, guys?'

The young Novu boy looked creased and ruffled, but better for his rest. His skin was its normal lilac colour and his turquoise eyes were wide and alert.

'Hello, shipmate,' said Jake. 'It's good to see you up and about.'

'How are you feeling?' asked Kella.

'I sore, but OK.' Nanoo glanced over their shoulders. 'We land on Shan-Ti? I not remember it being so white.'

The three of them watched the other passenger ships fill the crater, like huge metal sausages crammed into a giant frying pan.

A group of cyber-monks in grey robes emerged from the monastery, followed by several novices in white tunics. In front of them, Jake recognised the balding head, snowy beard and black robes of the cyber-abbot, Father Benedict.

'Come on,' he said. 'We had better go and say hello.'

Shan-Ti was a lot colder than it had been on their last visit and a thick layer of snow covered the crater surface. Captain Swan was waiting for them outside in a long white coat with his collar up and his cap pulled low.

As they set off for the monastery, they heard someone calling out their names on the wind. Jake spotted Crazy Kay Jagger chasing after them in her yellow combat spacesuit. It was common for pirate crews to wear their own colours, but not many of them sported a lace tutu and knee-high gravity boots. Kay was also the only pirate in the galaxy to carry a semi-automatic bubble gun and feather duster.

'Ahoy-hoy, shipmates,' she cheered. 'Did you miss me?'

When she caught up with them, Kay removed her helmet and flicked her nest of pink hair out of her eyes. Kella gasped in surprise. A web of scars stretched across one half of Kay's face, exploding outwards from a shiny black eyepatch.

'How you get injured?' asked Nanoo.

'It was a leaving present from Scarabus Shark,' she said, bitterly. 'I caught a face full of burning control panel when the *Divine Wind* collided with the *Black Death*. Now I'm blind in one eye. And I look like Granny Leatherhead.'

Jake found it hard not to stare as Kay ran a finger over her rutted cheek.

'Does it hurt?' he asked.

'No,' she said. 'It's weird. I can't feel a thing. That bit of my skin is totally numb.'

'Would you like me to heal it?' asked Kella.

Kay shook her head. 'It'll take more than a handful of crystals to fix this mess.'

'Maybe the cyber-monks can help,' said Jake, pointing to his own purple eye implants.

Kay glanced towards the monastery. 'Why would they help a spacejacker?'

'You never know until you ask,' he said, blowing into his cold hands. 'Come on, let's not keep our hosts waiting.'

The five of them proceeded towards the monastery, where the cyber-monks stood waiting. Father Benedict marched out to meet them, his black robes stirring up a flurry of snow.

'Jake Cutler,' he called out. 'What in the name of technology are you doing here?'

'Hello, father,' said Jake. 'We need your help.'

'I feared you were dead.' Father Benedict surveyed the gathering crowds. 'Who are those people?'

'They're independent colonists,' said Captain Swan. 'We were forced to flee Santanova after the explosion.'

'They're refugees?'

'Yes, can they stay here?' asked Jake. 'They need sanctuary and they have nowhere else to go.'

'Here?' Father Benedict looked pointedly around the crater. 'This is a monastery, a place of study and worship. How are we supposed to conceal such large spacecraft?'

'Don't worry about the ships,' said Jake. 'It's only the people who are staying.'

'We go off to fight war,' explained Nanoo. 'Jake is only leader who can stop Interstellar Government.'

Father Benedict looked horrified. 'You're going to take on the Interstellar Navy by yourselves? A captain, four children and a collection of passenger ships?'

Jake pulled himself up to full height. 'Actually, I have a plan to build my own fleet of warships, but I need your technology to make it work.'

Father Benedict squinted nervously at the sky. 'You had better come inside.'

The cyber-abbot led Jake and his friends through the tunnelled corridors of the monastery, which felt warm and dry compared to the crater. When they reached his office, Father Benedict offered them each a hot drink, before lowering himself into a wide chair behind a stone desk.

'It's not going to be easy to feed these people,' he warned. 'We barely grow enough food for ourselves.'

'We'll leave all the supplies we can spare,' said Captain Swan. 'Perhaps the Shan-Ti government would be willing to help with the rest.'

'Is that why you brought us inside, father?' asked Jake. 'To talk about food?'

'No.' Father Benedict checked the window and lowered his voice. 'I know what the Interstellar Government is planning.'

Chapter 3

Clicks and Whistles

'How you know what Interstellar Government planning?' asked Nanoo.

Father Benedict blushed like a naughty novice. 'We've used our technology to hack their naval communications. Ever since Jake left the planet, we've been intercepting messages from Admiral Vantard.'

'But that's against Interstellar Law,' said Kella.

'So is blowing up an entire city,' pointed out Jake.

'Did you know that they were planting a mega-bomb on Santanova?' asked Captain Swan, his eyes narrowing.

The cyber-abbot shook his head. 'No, it was never mentioned in any of the communications we hacked. But we do know that the Vantos incident was staged, not that anyone believed a lone planetary guard ship would intentionally attack a naval fleet. It seems that Admiral Vantard wanted an excuse to start trouble in the seventh solar system, because that's where the galactic war is supposed to start.'

'Supposed to?' queried Kella.

'Yes, the seventh is viewed as particularly trouble-some, mainly because that's where the *ISS Colossus* went missing. The Interstellar Navy will take control of the independent colonies there, before working their way back to the first. By the time the naval fleet reaches us here in the fourth, there won't be enough colonies left to stop them.'

'I bet the Interstellar Government has been plan-ning this for years,' said Jake angrily. 'Has there been any news about Vantos, or Santanova?'

'As far as we know, Santanova is holding out following the explosion, but it's not looking good for Vantos or its neighbours, Abbere and Torbana.' Father Benedict's expression turned grim. 'I don't know how much longer those colonies can last. If you're going to do something, you had better do it fast.'

'Has the Interstellar Navy attacked Reus?' asked Captain Swan anxiously. 'My crew are worried about their families.'

'Not yet,' said Father Benedict. 'But it's only a matter of time. As for the rest of the Interstellar Navy, most of the remaining warships are stirring up trouble in the second, third and fourth solar systems, while their special forces guard the first.'

'How about the fifth and sixth solar systems?' asked Kella eagerly.

'A few vessels have been left behind to protect the United Worlds in those solar systems,' said Father Benedict. 'However, the fighting in the seventh will soon spread.'

'What about the Gorks?' asked Kay.

Father Benedict cast a disapproving eye over her pink hair and space-pirate outfit. 'The Gorks have been given orders to terrorise the main trade routes between each solar system. But several Gork warships have been spotted heading to the sixth solar system.'

'We'll have to take out the naval fleet in the seventh solar system first,' said Jake, more to himself than anyone else in the room.

'How many ships it have?' asked Nanoo.

Jake tried to remember what he had once read. 'If this is a large fleet, it could have as many as ten naval warships –'

'It has twenty,' corrected Father Benedict. 'As well as thirty gunships and over two hundred fighter craft.'

Kella groaned. Naval gunships were smaller than warships, but they were faster and able to bear heavy laser cannon.

'What possible justification does the Interstellar Navy have for deploying that many ships to the seventh?' growled Captain Swan.

'The official story is that they were on a training exercise when they were attacked,' said Father Benedict. 'But no one is buying that, so Admiral Vantard is now claiming that the independent colonies in that solar system were planning to strike the United Worlds first.'

'That's garbish,' snapped Jake. 'If there was such a plan, it died on Santanova with all of the independent colony leaders.'

'All of them, except for the ruler of Altus.' Father Benedict eyed him curiously. 'And now you want to avenge their death. But how do you propose to build your fleet?'

'That's why I need your help,' said Jake. 'Without the stellar-net, we can use your technology to send a message to the independent colonies. It's our only hope of fighting back.'

'Which colonies?'

'All of them.'

Father Benedict considered this for a moment and then nodded. 'It won't be easy, but our satellites should be powerful enough, thanks to young Nanoo. Of course, we'll have to encrypt the message, so it can only be accessed by the colonies. And scramble the signal, so it cannot be traced back here, in case the message is intercepted.'

'How long will it take to reach the furthest planet?' asked Jake.

'It depends on solar conditions, but it could take a few hours, once we've programmed the satellites. But without the stellar-net, we'll have no way of knowing if the colonies have received your message and they won't be able to reply.'

There was a sharp knock at the door and a young novice entered the room.

'I'm sorry to interrupt, father,' he said, 'but the planetary guard is here.'

Jake checked the window and spotted two red camouflaged fighter craft hovering over the crater. Their powerful thrusters stirred up thick clouds of snow as their pilots surveyed the crowds. Father Benedict remained seated behind his desk.

'I wondered how long it would take for them to spot the passenger ships,' he said, pouring himself another drink. 'We are on high alert after all.'

'How shall I respond, father?' asked the novice.

'Tell them that we have refugees from Santanova and we need to talk urgently with the deputy prime minister.'

The novice left the room and Jake leant on the windowsill to watch the two fighters.

'What happens now?' he asked.

'The novices will attend to the refugees,' said Father Benedict, 'while the brothers prepare the satellites to send your message.'

'How long that take?' asked Nanoo, pouring his drink into one of his neck slits.

'Not long,' assured the cyber-abbot, using his skull implants to send out his instructions. 'In the meantime, I have something to show you.'

'What is it?' asked Jake.

Father Benedict picked up his handheld computer. 'It's a video message from your friends, Callidus and Capio. We received it before we lost the stellarnet signal.'

'They're alive?' Jake's heart leapt. 'I haven't seen them since before the gathering. They were supposed to meet us on Santanova.'

Father Benedict turned the screen towards them, which lit up to reveal the faces of Callidus and Capio. It seemed like years since Jake had seen the fortune seeker and his companion, both of whom looked tired and troubled.

'Ahoy, Shan-Ti monastery,' said Callidus. 'This is a message for Jake Cutler. Jake, I don't know if you and the others were on Santanova when the mega-bomb exploded, or if this message will ever reach you, but I pray that you are safe.'

Callidus spoke with surprising concern. It showed a sensitive side of him that Jake had rarely seen before. But then, the fortune seeker had changed since finding Altus.

'It's all kicking off here as well,' said Capio, pointing upwards. 'Gorks are attacking every independent colony ship they find.'

'That's why we were unable to meet you on Santanova,' explained Callidus. 'All of the passenger ships in the third solar system have been grounded for their own safety. We're trying to find someone willing to take us to Shan-Ti. If you get this message, wait for us at the monastery. We should be there within a couple of days.'

'Assuming we make it to you alive,' muttered Capio.

Callidus ignored him and stared into the camera. Jake could tell that there was something bothering the fortune seeker. His blue eyes looked sadder than he remembered.

'Jake, there's something important I need to tell you,' said Callidus. 'But it's not something I can say over the stellar-net. I hope we get to speak in person soon. In the meantime, keep an eye on the stars and –'

The screen went blank.

'Where's the rest of the message?' asked Jake.

'There is no more,' said Father Benedict, putting down the handheld computer. 'Because that's when we lost the stellar-net signal.'

Jake knew how the message was supposed to end. Callidus always said the same thing: *Keep an eye on the stars and stay out of trouble.* This sounded like excellent advice in the face of a galactic war, but Jake was about to do the exact opposite and seek out more trouble than he had ever imagined.

As he returned to the window, Jake felt a weight lift from his mind. Callidus and Capio were alive and they were making their way to Shan-Ti. He had missed them both and he could not wait to see them. Not only that, if anyone could help him to fight a war, it was Cal.

Kella looked thoughtful. 'I wonder what's so important that Callidus is worried someone else might hear it.'

'Perhaps he know way to stop Interstellar Navy,' ventured Nanoo. 'Like secret weapon.'

'In that case, I hope he gets here soon,' said Captain Swan. 'Because we need all the help we can get.'

'There's one more message. At least, we think it's a message.' Father Benedict tapped his handheld computer. 'This one didn't arrive over the stellar-net. It was picked up by one of our largest satellites early this morning.'

'Is it message from Novu people?' asked Nanoo, excitedly. 'My people reply?'

Father Benedict smiled and handed him the device. 'Yes, we think it came from Taan-Centaur, but it's hard to tell.'

Nearly two weeks ago, Nanoo had used the cyber-monk satellites to send his people a message, explaining how he had been stranded when his parents' exploration ship had crashed, killing them and the crew. It had taken a long time for the message to reach his home planet, Taan-Centaur, because it was located so far away.

Nanoo stared at the handheld computer with expectant eyes. No images appeared, only strange clicks and whistles muffled by static.

'What's that?' asked Kay.

'It's the Novu language,' said Jake.

The message lasted a few seconds before cutting out. Nanoo played it twice more and a wide grin spread across his lilac face.

'What did it say?' asked Kella.

'It from my Uncle Morc,' said Nanoo. 'He only say two words.'

'What were they?' asked Jake.

'We coming.'

There was a stunned silence.

'Does that mean your uncle is sending a rescue mission to get you?' asked Kella.

'I think it so,' said Nanoo. 'Uncle Morc is commander of many Novu ships. He must send one to pick up me.'

'He's an admiral?' Kay sounded impressed.

'Yes, but not same as Interstellar Navy,' he assured them. 'My uncle protect people, not attack them.'

'How long will it take for him to get here?' asked Jake.

'It depend on which ship he use, but maybe two weeks, three at most.'

'Is that all?' exclaimed Captain Swan. 'It would take the *Star Chaser* months to reach another galaxy, if not years.'

'That correct,' said Nanoo. 'But it quicker with Novu technology.'

'If the message took a week to reach us, then your uncle could be halfway here by now,' calculated Jake. 'That means you could be back on Taan-Centaur within a month.'

'I know,' said Nanoo. 'It not seem real after such long time.'

Kella smiled, but her voice betrayed a hint of sadness. 'You should wait for your uncle here on Shan-Ti.'

Nanoo thought about this for a moment and then shook his head. 'No, I help my friends stop Interstellar Navy first.'

'Are you crazy?' said Jake. 'There's no point risking your life for us, when you're so close to going home. This isn't your war.'

'Yes it is,' insisted Nanoo. 'I am proud spacejacker and my crew need me. You and Kella not run away, so I not go home until we save seven solar systems. I making it my war.'

The Novu boy folded his arms and turned his head to indiciate that he had made up his mind.

'OK,' said Jake, with a mixture of respect and incredulity. 'I think you're barmy, but thank you, shipmate.'

A light flashed on Father Benedict's handheld computer. The cyber-abbot picked it up and smiled at Jake.

'The satellites have been prepared. Are you ready to send your message?'

Chapter 4

A Message of Hope

Jake took a deep breath and nodded. 'I'm ready.'

'Good,' said Father Benedict. 'We had better hurry before the stellar-net is restored.'

'Why would that make a difference?' asked Kella.

'It would just be better for Jake to send his message to the independent colonies before …' The cyber-abbot's smile slipped.

'Before what?' Jake was confused.

Father Benedict shifted awkwardly. 'We discovered that the Interstellar Government is going to blame you for the mega-bomb on Santanova. As soon as the stellar-net is restored, Admiral Vantard will tell the galaxy that the explosion was an act of terrorism.'

'But I had nothing to do with that bomb,' protested Jake.

'I know that,' said Father Benedict. 'But how do you think it will look to the other colonies? After all, it was you who requested the gathering and you who left the city moments before the explosion. It would be easier for people to blame a space pirate than go to war. If we don't get your message to the colonies first, we might not convince any of them to follow you.'

Jake picked up a pencil and notepad from the desk. 'So what are we waiting for?'

Father Benedict connected a microphone to his handheld computer, while Jake sat scribbling notes. It reminded him of writing the speech for the gathering, only this time the words seemed to come more easily. Kella stood behind his chair and read the notepad over his shoulder.

'We need a name,' she said.

'What do you mean?'

'Well, we can't keep referring to ourselves as refugees or space pirates. We need something official that will inspire our allies and frighten our enemies.'

'How about the Star Slayers?' Kay spread the imaginary words out in front of her.

'It has … spirit,' said Captain Swan tactfully. 'But I suspect that the independent colonies would respond better to something a little more – how do I put it? – dignified.'

Kay scowled and stormed over to the window.

'I've got it,' said Jake. 'We can call ourselves the Independent Alliance.'

Kella wrinkled her nose. 'It's not very exciting.'

'And it's not nearly scary enough,' grumbled Kay.

'But it's what we are,' said Jake enthusiastically. 'We're an alliance of colonies fighting to keep our independence. It's perfect.'

Nanoo smiled. 'That name work for me.'

The others nodded their approval.

'That's agreed,' said Jake cheerily. 'We're the Independent Alliance.'

Father Benedict cleared his throat. 'I'm glad that's sorted, because we're ready to record.'

As though by magic, the room fell silent. Jake checked his notes, cleared his throat and leant over the microphone. Across the desk, Father Benedict pressed the 'record' button and held up his thumb. Jake spoke slowly and confidently, as though he had rehearsed the words a hundred times.

'This is a message of hope for the independent colonies. My name is Jake Cutler and I am the ruler of Altus. Following the detonation of a mega-bomb on Santanova, we are now at war. The Interstellar Government has murdered our leaders and its navy is attacking our homes. Why? Because the galaxy is facing a serious crystal shortage. The Interstellar Government wants to turn our planets into United Worlds, so the Galactic Trade Corporation can rip up our surfaces in search of more crystals. If we do not act now, our colonies will be wiped out.'

Jake paused for dramatic effect.

'The danger is real and fighting has already broken out in the seventh solar system. If you choose to stand alone, your planet will fall. We must unite and fight the Interstellar Navy together, as an Independent Alliance. It's only through our combined strength that we can hope to defeat them. Your leaders signed a treaty before they died. It was destroyed in the explosion that killed them, but the alliance remains. Do not let their deaths be in vain. I'm asking you to stand with me and build the greatest battle fleet of independent ships ever known.'

Jake let the words hang for a moment before finishing his message.

'I already have vessels from Santanova and Reus, but we will need more to defeat the Interstellar Navy. Please do not underestimate this historic moment, my fellow colonists. The freedom of our planets and the lives of our people are at stake. We must not allow the Interstellar Government to sell our homes for blood crystals. If you value your independence, send as many ships as you can spare to support the Independent Alliance. We'll meet at Libertina in the sixth solar system in five days' time, before

45

heading into battle in the seventh. If it's war the Interstellar Government wants, it's war they will get.'

Jake held his breath while Father Benedict stopped the recording. His pulse was racing and his hands shook with excitement.

'Well done,' said Father Benedict, scooping up the handheld computer. 'I'll get this message sent out straight away.'

As he left the room, Kay raised her hands in wonder. 'That was incredible, shipmate. You're a natural leader.'

Jake smiled. 'Not bad for a spacejacker, eh?'

'It's a good idea to meet the other ships at Libertina, before we enter the seventh solar system together,' said Kella. 'I just can't believe we have to wait five days. How many planets will have fallen by then?'

'We should leave now.' Kay started for the door. 'If we hurry, we can be there sooner.'

'I applaud your enthusiasm, but we can't leave yet,' said Captain Swan. 'It will take us at least two days to repair the *Divine Wind* and make the passenger ships battleworthy. But that's beside the point, because it will still take some of the furthest colonies a full five days to reach Libertina. We'll only get one shot at saving the seventh solar system and therefore we'll need all of the ships we can get.'

Jake knew the captain was right, but it didn't make him feel any better. He wondered if his words were already making their way through space. How many ships would the other colonies send? There was no way of knowing until they reached Libertina. All that Jake could do now was prepare the convoy for battle.

Father Benedict returned to the room, looking flustered. 'The deputy prime minister has arrived.'

A squadron of red fighters circled the crater, while three shiny shuttle craft landed in front of the monastery. Jake watched through the window as planetary guards from the first two shuttles secured the area, before the door of the third shuttle opened and a set of steps unfolded. A short woman in a vibrant yellow coat emerged and surveyed the winter scene. Jake could make out her sharp features below a fur-trimmed hood.

Kristina Lemark observed the crowds sheltering beneath the passenger ships, while someone held an umbrella above her head. When the deputy prime minister was ready, she walked over to the monastery, paying no attention to the tangle of assistants who fussed around her.

A few minutes later, the office door opened and armed planetary guards entered. Jake remained still as they scanned the room and parted way for Kristina Lemark. It was now so crowded that Jake found himself backed up against the window. Father Benedict stood to greet the new arrivals.

'Welcome, deputy prime minister,' he said, bobbing his head respectfully. 'Let me introduce you to our visitors.'

Kristina's eyes flicked curiously around the room until they found the face that they were searching for.

'It's Jake Cutler, isn't it?' she said.

'That's right. Ruler of Altus.' Jake stepped forward and shook her hand.

'Altus?' she repeated.

Jake detected the doubt in her voice.

'I know it sounds like garbish,' he said. 'But Altus does exist and it's the most independent colony in the seven solar systems.'

'So where is it?'

'I can't tell you, not until I know that my people are safe from the Interstellar Government. Space pirates from Zerost discovered Altus centuries ago and it has remained hidden ever since. If you need proof, my uniform contains the symbol of Altus, my gold pendant is the seal of Altus, and this cutlass is the sword of Altus.'

Jake drew the weapon and held it up to the light. The planetary guards reacted by raising their laser rifles, but Kristina signalled for them to hold fire, while Jake resheathed his sword.

'How did you survive the explosion?' she asked.

Jake told her about the Altian traitor, Jorge Dasch, who had lured him away from the gathering with a mysterious note, before trying to sell him out to Admiral Vantard. 'The Interstellar Government planted the mega-bomb and now they're going to wipe out the independent colonies.'

'That's a very serious allegation,' she said. 'And not one that can be easily proved. Do you have any evidence?'

'No, but who else would kill our leaders and attack our planets? Whether we like it or not, we're already at war with the United Worlds and by the time the fighting reaches Shan-Ti, it will be too late to stop their Interstellar Navy.'

The more senior guards broke into frantic muttering. Jake tried to speak, but his words were lost in the incoherent chatter.

'Silence, you dogs,' cried Kay, leaping on to a chair with her sword drawn.

The guards jumped back and took aim with their laser rifles, but Jake quickly stepped in front of Kay with his hands raised. Kristina Lemark ordered her people to stand down and the room fell silent. Kay resheathed her sword, blew a kiss and hopped down from the chair.

Jake glanced around the office to make sure that he had everyone's attention. 'Will you help us to fight the Interstellar Navy, deputy prime minister?'

Kristina Lemark tapped her thin lips with the tips of her fingers. Jake held his breath as he waited for her to speak.

'What do you need?' she asked.

'All the Shan-Ti ships you can spare,' he said. 'We're going to build a fleet to fight the Interstellar Navy in the seventh solar system.'

'And then what?'

'We'll keep fighting, until we take down the Interstellar Government.'

The deputy prime minister raised her eyebrows. 'I applaud your bravery, Mr Cutler. However, my first priority is to protect this planet and its colonists, as well as the refugees you brought here.'

'What does that mean?'

'I'm sorry,' she said. 'But we cannot spare any of our ships.'

Jake stared at the deputy prime minister in surprise. Next to him, Kella and Nanoo appeared equally as shocked. It took Jake a moment to find his voice.

'But we have to stop the Interstellar Navy,' he insisted, trying his best to keep calm.

'This fleet that you're building,' said Kristina Lemark irritably. 'How many warships do you have at your command?'

Jake gritted his teeth. 'None, but –'

'And gunships?'

'None, but I've sent a message to the other colonies and I'm hoping that they will send some to meet us.'

'Hoping?' The deputy prime minister regarded him with hawkish eyes. 'If you want to throw away your life on a suicide mission with only a few passenger ships and a handful of fighter craft, that is your choice, Mr Cutler. I'm afraid that I cannot sacrifice my planetary guards based on your hopes.'

With that, Kristina Lemark turned and swept out of the office.

'Hey, wait –' Jake attempted to follow, but his path was blocked by the guards.

'Let her go,' said Father Benedict. 'I expect that she needs time to think about it. No one likes the idea of war.'

Chapter 5

The Fire

Jake, Kella and Nanoo worked tirelessly with the cyber-monks and crews to prepare the passenger ships for war. Nanoo showed them how to boost the engines and increase the shield strength, while the cyber-monks helped to install the new laser cannon and torpedo tubes, which they had salvaged from old planetary guard vessels. By the end of the second day, the twelve ships resembled fierce battlecraft.

Jake finished sealing a large metal plate on to the side of the *Star Chaser* and climbed down to admire his work. He hoped that the modifications would be enough to fend off a naval warship. His thoughts were interrupted when a shower of pearlesque bubbles drifted past him. He glanced up to see Kay standing on top of the frosted hull, holding her semi-automatic bubble gun.

'Ahoy-hoy, Kid Cutler,' she called out. 'The light is fading fast and everyone is freezing, so we're going to start a campfire and sing some space shanties. Do you want to join us?'

Jake switched off his laser cutter and nodded. 'That sounds good to me.'

The refugee camp was based in the middle of the crater, under the shade of the passenger ships. As Jake and Kay entered a circle of large canvas tents, they spotted Kella and Nanoo, who had been working on the fighter craft.

'How's it going?' asked Kella.

'Great,' said Jake. 'The passenger ships look as hard as diamonds.'

'You should see what Nanoo has done to the fighters. I've never known ships to move so fast.'

Nanoo blushed dark lilac. 'It nothing.'

Jake was not surprised. Nanoo had previously used his technical skills to improve the *Dark Horse*. He had also built several devices out of spare parts, including a lie detector, a radio-wave blocker and a laserproof vest.

'I wish the *Divine Wind* was ready,' said Kay. 'My crew has replaced most of the hull plates, but there's still a lot to do before we can launch.'

'Are they joining us tonight?' asked Jake.

'Not likely,' she huffed. 'All they do is moan about this place. I can't blame them really; the Luna

Ticks want to spacejack passenger ships, not make them tougher. My first mate reckons that the *Divine Wind* is cursed and we should leave it here to rust in the snow.'

Kay led Jake, Kella and Nanoo to a clearing, where someone had stacked a pile of broken furniture from the passenger ships. The temperature was dropping fast and Jake was glad when the fire was lit.

A few of the colonists had managed to rustle up some stellar-burgers and corn-cakes, which they laid out on a huge metal grill near the flames. This would be the last night on the surface for the crews and they were making it special. Jake wished that Callidus and Capio could have been there to share the moment. Why was it taking them so long to reach Shan-Ti? He didn't want to leave without them, but the convoy could not wait.

As people warmed themselves by the fire, Jake spotted Father Benedict in the crowd. The cyberabbot rushed over to where they were standing.

'I bring good news,' he said, jovially. 'Kristina Lemark is so impressed with the progress we're making on the passenger ships, she's now prepared to commit two of the Shan-Ti warships to your fleet, assuming that she can find enough volunteers to crew them.'

'Two?' Kay looked scandalised. 'Is that all?'

'It's two more than you have now.'

Jake smiled. 'It's a start.'

'Precisely,' said Father Benedict. 'Who knows how many more ships will join the Independent Alliance in the days to come?'

Jake gazed up at the darkening sky.

'You had better watch out, Interstellar Government,' he whispered. 'We're coming for you.'

As the evening drew on, Jake watched the flames lick the night sky, while blackened wood crackled and popped on the frosty ground. It was hard for him not to think of the burning monastery on Remota, where the cyber-monks had been killed by naval troops in disguise. However, instead of deafening plasma rifles and palm grenades, the crater was filled with a cheery chorus of space shanties.

Kella crouched next to him, chomping a char-grilled stellar-burger. A few of the colonists had started to dance in front of the fire. Nanoo joined them, flinging his long lilac arms about in time with the music.

'Do you think I should say something?' asked Jake. 'You know, a few words to inspire the crews.'

'It wouldn't hurt,' said Kella. 'But you should wait until they've finished singing and dancing.'

Jake nodded. 'Mind you, what can I say to re-assure them? For all we know, the other colonies might not send any ships.'

Kella chewed a mouthful of stellar-burger. 'Would that stop you from fighting the Interstellar Navy?'

'No, but it would make it much harder to beat them.' Jake picked at his own stellar-burger. 'If only there were a way to rescue the Space Dogs. We could really use their experience and the *Dark Horse* is a tough old ship.'

'I'm not sure the Luna Ticks would be too keen on that idea,' she said. 'How many times have they saved the Space Dogs already? It used to be every space pirate for themselves.'

Jake chuckled. 'You thought that I was a space pirate when we first met. Do you remember?'

Kella smirked. 'And you thought that I was stuck-up, but it turns out that you're from the richest planet in the seven solar systems. It's like something out of a space tale, where the poor orphan boy finds out that he's actually a wealthy pirate prince.'

'I'm not an orphan,' he protested, causing several people to glance in his direction. 'My dad is still out there, waiting for me.'

Kella realised what she had said. 'Yes, of course, sorry. Do you think he saw you on the *Interstellar News*?'

Jake shrugged. 'I figured that he would come out of hiding if he knew about the galactic war, but now I don't know what to think. My dad is supposed to be this great hero, so what's he waiting for?'

'Listen, Jake, don't take this the wrong way, but why do you want to find him so badly? I mean, you've survived this long without him and you've turned out OK. In fact, better than OK. You're the most senior colonist in the galaxy.'

'It's hard to explain.' Jake stared into the flames. 'There has always been something missing in my life. I've never had parents. If only I can find my dad, I might finally understand who I am and perhaps the universe will make more sense. Without him, I feel so alone.'

'But you're not alone, you're a Space Dog. We're in this together. It's just that the galaxy is such a big place. What if you never find your dad? How do you even know that Jorge Dasch was telling the truth about seeing him? After all, he was a traitor and I've never even heard of head-cuffs. What I'm trying to say is be careful not to miss what you already have around you.'

The final space shanty ended and the crater fell silent. Jake realised that it was time for him to say something inspirational. But as he climbed to his feet,

Kay rushed forward with her bubble gun and took aim at the fire. A cloud of oily orbs flew out of the barrel and ignited on the flames in a series of bright flashes. Jake realised that she must have added some sort of fuel or chemical to the bubble mixture. The colonists cheered at the firework display and Kay howled like a wild animal.

'That girl should have her own show on the stellar-net,' said Jake.

Kay winked at him as she held up a balloon. It was full of the same oily substance as her bubble gun and it wobbled precariously in her hand. Jake realised what she was about to do, but before he could stop her, she hurled the balloon into the fire, where it burst into a huge fireball. He turned his face away as a wave of heat washed over them.

'Watch it!' shouted Kella.

'Are you OK?' asked Jake.

'Yeah, fine, but if she's not careful, someone is going to get hurt.'

As Jake opened his mouth to reply, there was an even bigger explosion and this time flames shot high into the sky.

'That's enough!' he said, but as he looked up, he realised that Kay wasn't responsible. His eyes scanned the surface for the source of the fire.

'Over there,' cried Kella. 'A ship is on fire.'

Kay screamed with rage. 'It's the *Divine Wind*!'

Jake's first thought was that they were under attack, but the sky was clear. He realised that it must have been an accident, perhaps a ruptured fuel tank or exploding laser cannon. Kay charged off towards her ship, still clutching her bubble gun.

'Come on,' said Jake, signalling to Kella and Nanoo. 'We've got to help her.'

While most people stood and stared, Jake sprinted off through the snow after Kay. He wasn't particularly strong, but he had always been fast. As they raced through the tents, he spotted the cyber-monks and novices carrying buckets of water, which he doubted would be enough to stop the fire spreading to the rest of the fleet. How else could they put it out? Apart from the monastery, there was no water in the crater and none of the ships were equipped with hoses.

Jake reached the *Divine Wind* first and skidded to a halt in the melting snow. He instinctively raised his hands and turned away from the intense heat. Kay stopped next to him, tears streaming from her good eye.

'My ship,' she panted. 'We have to save it.'

Jake watched as novices splashed water on to the flames, but they might as well have blown on them, for all the good it did. The fire flared suddenly and Jake pulled Kay back to a safe distance. He retched as gritty black smoke tickled his throat.

'We've got to get inside the ship,' he said.

Kay frowned. 'Inside?'

Kella and Nanoo arrived behind them, gasping for breath.

'We have to fly the *Divine Wind* into space,' said Jake. 'The lack of oxygen will choke the flames. It's the only way to put out the fire and save the fleet.'

'You're not serious?' wheezed Kella, her hands resting on her knees.

Nanoo glanced nervously at the burning ship. 'That sound dangerous.'

'It's the only way,' insisted Jake. 'There are no flames underneath the ship and the loading ramp is open. All we have to do is get inside the cargo hold and we'll be protected from the heat.'

'You make it sound easy,' said Kella.

'But *Divine Wind* not ready,' pointed out Nanoo. 'New hull plates not tested.'

'It's a risk we'll have to take,' said Jake. 'We can't afford to lose a ship or let the fire spread.'

Kay grinned at him. 'Let's do it.'

As the fire intensified, Jake darted into the nearest tent and located four thick blankets. He stopped a novice carrying two buckets and used the water to douse the material.

'Here, put these over your head,' he said, passing wet blankets to his friends. 'And follow me.'

Jake threw the heavy fabric over himself and felt the icy water soak into his hair and clothes. With only the ground beneath his feet visible, he stumbled blindly towards the *Divine Wind*. All that he could hear was the roar of the flames and his gravity boots scuffing the rocky surface. After several steps, he chanced a peek, but regretted it when the heat scorched his face and the smoke filled his lungs.

'We're almost there,' he coughed. 'Keep going.'

It was like walking into a giant furnace. But before long, Jake reached the shadow of the star frigate and his feet hit the hot loading ramp. He scrambled into the safety of the cargo hold and threw off his smoking blanket. Kay was next, followed by Nanoo, whose blanket had caught fire. Jake helped to beat out the flames on the grated floor.

'Where's Kella?' he asked.

Kay and Nanoo looked frantically around, but Kella was not behind them.

Chapter 6

Night Flight

Jake snatched up his blanket and flung it over his head. He charged back down the loading ramp and retraced his steps. In desperation, his sore eyes searched the surface for Kella, but it was difficult to see clearly in the heat haze. He staggered a few more paces and found her curled up on the ground, with molten metal raining down around her.

There was no time to check if Kella was OK. Jake grabbed her arms and dragged her back to the loading ramp, where Kay and Nanoo were waiting to haul her to safety. As her charred shoes disappeared inside, Jake pulled himself into the cargo hold with his blistered hands and closed the ramp.

'Is she alive?' asked Kay.

Nanoo pulled off the remains of the blanket. Kella lay on the floor with her eyes closed. Her skin was badly burnt and blackened by the smoke. Nanoo bent over and placed his ear by her mouth. His wide turquoise eyes bulged with concern as he listened intently.

'Kella alive,' he said. 'But she need help.'

Jake held up his gold pendant. 'Can you use the crystals to heal her?'

Nanoo shook his head. 'I not know how, but I will take her to medical bay and see what I can do. Just hurry and launch ship, Kay.'

'Me?' exclaimed the teenage pirate captain. 'I don't know how to fly this thing.'

'What?' Jake stared at her.

'I'm sorry,' she said. 'I've never trained to be a pilot. I have no idea how to launch this ship.'

Jake forgot about his blistered hands and jumped to his feet. 'Is that supposed to be funny?'

'It's not a joke. I can't even fly a hover-bike.'

'What we do?' asked Nanoo. 'I only know how to fly Novu craft and no time to fetch more people.'

'I'll launch the ship,' said Jake. 'I've done loads of simulations and I once flew a naval shuttle.'

'This is a lot bigger than a shuttle,' pointed out Kay.

Jake opened the inner hatch. 'Well, it's either me or the fire.'

Nanoo carefully picked up Kella in his long arms and carried her to the medical bay, while Jake and Kay rushed to the bridge.

'Can you really fly a star frigate?' asked Kay when they reached the top deck.

'We're about to find out,' said Jake.

The bridge was soaked in orange light from the flame-filled windows. Jake strapped himself into the pilot's seat and switched on the power. The control panel flickered to life and rows of red dots flashed at him. An external temperature gauge shot well past the danger line and an old-fashioned siren bleated overhead.

'We must be barking mad,' laughed Kay, strapping herself into the captain's chair, which was positioned below a shelf of pink skull-shaped helmets.

Jake pressed a switch labelled *Intercom* and spoke into the microphone. 'Nanoo, get yourself and Kella strapped in quick, we're about to take off.'

With a quick glance at Kay, he started the engine. It rumbled to life and Jake felt the entire ship shake, as though it were waking from a nightmare. He checked his instruments, most of which looked similar to those on the *Dark Horse*.

'Are you OK?' asked Kay.

'Yeah, sure,' he said, trying to remember everything that he had ever read about star frigates. 'Just getting myself acquainted with your ship.'

The intercom speaker crackled.

'We in medical bay and strapped in tight,' confirmed Nanoo.

'Great,' said Jake, punching several buttons and gripping the controls. 'Let's put out this fire.'

The blast of the exhausts thundered over the roar of the flames. Jake could feel the power of the engine straining to be unleashed. Kay was right, this was nothing like a naval shuttle.

'What are you waiting for?' she asked.

Jake took the deepest breath of his life and released the thrusters. With the force of an explosion, the *Divine Wind* shot forward and Jake was thrown back in his seat. He held on to the controls as the ship bumped across the rocky surface, before it soared into the air. The flames whipped wildly outside the window and Jake caught glimpses of solid black.

'That's odd,' he said. 'Where are all the stars?'

There was nothing ahead except for darkness. It reminded him of the black hole that had swallowed Admiral Nex and the *ISS Colossus*. But then the light of the fire caught on something rough and uneven.

'It's the crater wall,' cried Kay. 'Pull up!'

The *Divine Wind* had not climbed high enough to clear the wall, which was blocking out the night sky. Jake wrenched back the controls and felt the nose of the star frigate rise sharply. A sea of stars crept into view as the ship tilted upwards.

'We're not going to make it,' warned Kay.

'Yes we are,' said Jake, straining with effort.

The *Divine Wind* was almost vertical when it reached the crater wall. Jake felt the rear of the ship hit the snow-covered rocks. There was a deep buckling sound like a giant cello as metal collided with stone, before the ship broke free and catapulted into the sky.

'Any damage?' asked Kay, as they left the surface behind.

Jake checked his instruments. 'As far as I can tell, the hull is still intact, but it looks as though we've lost an exhaust.'

The *Divine Wind* climbed higher into the atmosphere and Jake felt his body lighten with zero gravity. He eased off the thrusters and let the star frigate glide into space. Away from the planet, the controls felt more natural and the ship responded to his every movement. The flames outside the window started to wither and choke without oxygen.

'It's working,' said Kay, clapping her hands in delight. 'You had better switch on the artificial-gravity system.'

'Aye, captain.'

Kay activated the intercom. 'How are you two doing in the medical bay?'

'That not smoothest launch ever,' complained Nanoo. 'But we still in one piece. Is fire out?'

Jake got up and checked the nearest window. 'Aye, not a flame in sight.'

'How's the hull look?' asked Kay.

Jake squinted through the frosted glass. 'It'll need a good clean and a new coat of paint, but otherwise it's –'

Crack!

There was a noise like breaking ice and a thin line appeared in the glass beneath Jake's cheek. He jumped back and stared at the fracture, his heart pounding.

'Get away from there,' hissed Kay.

Jake remained where he was, his eyes fixed on the window. The glass was tough, but the sudden drop in temperature had weakened it.

'It's OK,' he said. 'It has stopped.'

Crack!

'There's another one.' Kay pointed to a side window, where a lightning-shaped streak had appeared. 'We had better get this ship back to the surface before one of them gives way.'

'Aye, captain.'

Jake returned to the pilot's seat and pulled hard on the controls. The *Divine Wind* swung back towards the crater, which was now only a small dot on the distant surface. A new warning light flashed on his display screen.

'What's that?' he asked.

'There's another vessel approaching.' Kay stared out of the front window. 'It looks like one of the passenger ships. We should try to dock with it, so we can get off this wreck and tow its worthless hull back to the surface.'

Jake had never docked with another vessel in space, but this didn't matter, because the passenger ship had other ideas.

'It's not slowing down,' he said. 'What's that crew playing at?'

Kay cursed. 'They must think we're OK, now that the fire is out.'

The passenger ship soared past the window and disappeared from view. Jake recognised it as the *Titanicus*, one of the most advanced vessels in the fleet.

'Do you want me to contact them?' he asked.

'Don't bother,' she moaned. 'It'll be quicker to land.'

Jake eased the *Divine Wind* back into the planet's atmosphere and squinted at the crater below. It was not unlike the simulations on the stellar-net. OK, a few of the controls were different, but he could do this, he could land the ship.

Crack!

One of the damaged windows threatened to collapse under the pressure of re-entry.

'How much further?' asked Kay.

'We're still in the stratosphere,' said Jake. 'It will be a few minutes before we –'

Crack!

The other window fractured so badly it looked like a spider's web. How many other windows were cracking throughout the ship? He tried not to think about the medical bay.

'Jake …'

'I know, I know.'

Heat and sparks glanced off the scorched hull as the *Divine Wind* plunged through the atmosphere. How much more punishment could the old star frigate take?

Kay activated the intercom. 'Hold on tight, Nanoo. We're coming in fast.'

'Come on,' muttered Jake to himself. 'Just a little bit further.'

CRASH!

A side window exploded in a shower of glass. Jake turned his face away as the atmospheric heat flooded the bridge.

'Here, catch,' shouted Kay, throwing him a pink skull-shaped helmet.

Jake caught the helmet and pulled it on to his head. It was a loose fit and he struggled to see through the protective mesh that covered the eye sockets, but at least it shielded his face. Kay donned her own helmet and gripped her seat straps.

A new warning light flashed on the control panel.

'Blast it,' said Jake. 'We're losing oxygen.'

The air became thin and bitter with sulphur. Jake found it hard to breathe inside his helmet. He tried to concentrate on the crater below, but he was becoming light-headed and his fingers were numbing fast.

'I can't … feel my …' slurred Kay, as she fought to stay conscious.

'Hold on,' he wheezed. 'We're entering the troposphere. I can see clear skies ahead.'

The heat of re-entry faded and fresh air poured through the open window. Jake wrenched off his helmet and filled his lungs with the wonderful ice-cold oxygen. His head cleared and his eyes fixed on the crater below, which was illuminated by the light of the fire. There wasn't much room for him to land the *Divine Wind* amongst the other ships, but what other choice did he have? It wasn't as though they could return to space with a broken window.

'Kay, contact the surface and tell everyone to stand clear,' he said, but there was no reply. 'Kay? Kay?'

The teenage pirate captain had passed out. Jake checked the control panel and flipped three switches to lower the landing gear. In the crater, he could make out a narrow clearing between two of the passenger ships. It looked wide enough to fit the *Divine Wind*, but it would be tight.

Jake slowed the star frigate and activated the docking thrusters. He eased the old ship into the crater and levelled off at the last second, as the other pilots had done on their arrival. The *Divine Wind* hovered precariously in the air above the clearing, while tents blew over and people scattered in all directions. Jake checked his position and carefully lowered the ship.

'Come on,' he muttered under his breath. 'You can do it.'

The thrusters screamed louder as the ship neared the ground and Jake braced for impact. He felt the landing gear connect heavily with the snow-covered surface and he eased off the thrusters. When he finally let go of the controls, his hands remained locked in a hooked position, like claws.

'Nice landing,' said a voice behind him.

Jake twisted around. 'I thought that you were out cold.'

Kay removed her pink skull-shaped helmet. 'I was, but I woke up in time to see you set this old space tub down. Not bad, shipmate.'

'Thanks,' said Jake modestly. 'Flying is much easier when you can see out of the windows.'

'I mean it,' she insisted. 'There are loads of pilots who would have messed that up. I reckon you're gifted with those controls.'

On any other day, Jake would have been thrilled to hear that, but there was no time to congratulate himself for saving the *Divine Wind*. Kella was hurt and she needed a medic.

Chapter 7

Mutiny

Kella was still unconscious when Jake and Kay reached the medical bay. Nanoo had smeared a thick, foul-smelling yellow ointment over her face and hands, but Jake could still make out patches of charred skin. Her shallow breaths rattled uneasily inside her chest as Nanoo stroked her burnt hair.

'How bad is she?' asked Kay.

'I not know,' said Nanoo. 'I find this cream for burns, but Kella not wake up.'

'Can we move her?' asked Jake.

Nanoo shrugged.

'We could fetch a medic,' suggested Kay.

'No offence,' said Jake, 'but the *Star Chaser* has a much better medical bay.'

The three of them carefully lifted Kella on to a rubber stretcher and carried her down to the cargo hold. Kay lowered the loading ramp and they were greeted by cheers. A crowd of colonists and cyber-monks had gathered around the ship.

'We need a medic,' shouted Jake. 'Kella is hurt.'

Several people rushed forward and took hold of the stretcher, including the medic from the *Star Chaser*. Jake watched anxiously as they carried her away.

'She's in good hands,' said Captain Swan reassuringly.

Father Benedict stared at the star frigate in astonishment. 'I can't believe that you used space to put the fire out. That was the bravest thing I've ever seen.'

'It was stupid and reckless,' scolded a familiar voice. 'And they're lucky to be alive.'

Jake scanned the crowd to see who had spoken. He recognised a tall figure with dark wavy hair.

'Cal!'

The fortune seeker made his way forward, tailed by his curly-haired companion, Capio. 'I thought that I told you to keep an eye on the stars and stay out of trouble.'

'Where have you been?' asked Jake, relieved to see his friend. 'We nearly had to leave without you.'

'I'm sorry it took so long,' said Callidus. 'We ended up catching a lift with a crew of smugglers, who kept changing course to avoid naval patrols. But we arrived in time to see who started the fire.'

'Who?' Kay drew her sword and glared at the crowd. 'Who dared to torch my father's ship?'

'It was a crew of pirates in yellow combat space-suits,' said Callidus. 'We were too far away to stop them.'

'The Luna Ticks?' Jake was confused. 'But that's Kay's own crew.'

Kay's freckled skin turned chalk white and for a moment it looked as though she was going to be sick, but then she recovered herself and roared with rage. 'Mutiny!'

'Yes, it looks that way,' said Callidus.

'Never trust a space pirate,' muttered Capio sagely.

'Where are those double-crossing dung-heads?' Kay looked wildly around the crater. 'I'll kill them.'

'Gone,' said Callidus. 'The fire was a distraction, so they could steal one of the passenger ships.'

'The *Titanicus*.' Jake clapped a hand to his fore-head. 'We passed it in space. The Luna Ticks have taken one of the best ships in the fleet.'

Kay shook her sword at the sky. 'We can't let them get away with it.'

'We won't,' said Jake, sharing her anger. 'But there's nothing we can do about it right now.'

'What do you mean, *nothing*?' snapped Kay. 'We can go after them. If we're going to take on the Interstellar Navy, we'll need the *Titanicus*.'

'And how do you propose we catch the Luna Ticks, if they have one of our fastest ships?' asked Captain Swan. 'Even if we could match their speed, do you think they would surrender without a fight? We might end up losing more than one vessel in a space battle.'

'That's a good point,' said Callidus. 'We're better off cutting our losses.'

'Cowards,' hissed Kay.

As much as Jake wanted to hunt down the traitors, he knew that they could not risk losing any more ships.

'I'm sorry, Kay,' he said. 'We will find those mutinous mongrels and we will make them pay for what they have done. But they will have to wait. The Interstellar Government is our top priority.'

Kay threw him a furious look and stormed back inside the *Divine Wind*, shouting over her shoulder.

'Blast the lot of you.'

The morning sun crept over the edge of the crater, casting long shadows across the fresh snow. Most people slept as a gentle breeze stroked their tents. The loading ramp of the *Divine Wind* remained firmly closed, as it had done all night.

Inside the *Star Chaser* medical bay, Jake and Nanoo took it in turns to watch over Kella. Her skin had been treated with a special laser, but it still looked red and swollen.

Callidus entered the room and approached the bed where Kella lay sleeping. His sharp blue eyes examined her wounded face and burnt clothes. As he swept back his hair, Jake noticed the metal lumps on the sides of his head, which someone had implanted before Callidus had lost his memory.

'Any change?' asked the fortune seeker.

'Not really.' Jake stifled a yawn. 'Her breathing has eased, but she's not showing any sign of waking up. It's going to take weeks for her burns to heal, if not months, and there's a good chance that she'll end up scarred.'

'I'm sorry to hear that,' said Callidus. 'But it could have been much worse.'

Jake groaned. 'I know. The whole thing was my idea. If she had died, it would have been my fault.'

'That's the burden of leadership. When you make a decision, it can sometimes mean that people get hurt. You had better get used to it, if you're going to lead these ships to war.' Callidus placed a hand on Nanoo's shoulder. 'Do you mind if I borrow Jake? I need to talk with him outside.'

'Not problem,' said Nanoo. 'I keeping my eyes on Kella.'

Jake wondered if Callidus was going to give him a lecture about staying out of trouble. He followed the fortune seeker into the crater, where the only sound was the snow crunching under their boots. As they walked, clouds of breath billowed from their mouths like smoke.

'You've been busy,' said Callidus, admiring the battle-ready passenger ships. 'I saw your speech at the gathering on Santanova. It was broadcast live across the *Interstellar News*. You've come a long way since we first met. There aren't many people who could unite the independent colonies.'

Jake shrugged. 'It was their fear of the Interstellar Navy that united them. Most of the leaders laughed when I first mentioned Altus.'

Callidus shifted uncomfortably at the name. The fortune seeker had spent years searching for the planet, but when he had finally stepped on to its surface in the light of the three crystal moons, the experience had overwhelmed him. After helping Jake defeat his Uncle Kear, Callidus had returned to the *Dark Horse* for the duration of their stay.

'Father Benedict told me about your plan. What you're doing is very courageous, but war is a dangerous business. Have you thought this through?'

'I've thought of nothing else,' said Jake. 'If we don't stop the Interstellar Government, millions of people will die.'

'So why head to the seventh solar system? Why not go straight to the Interstellar Government on Domus in the first solar system?'

'The independent colonies in the seventh urgently need our help. Their planets are surrounded by the Interstellar Navy and some of them are already under attack.' Jake kicked the snow. 'It's my fault their leaders are dead. If I hadn't contacted the mayor of Remota, there would never have been a gathering.'

Callidus considered this for a moment. 'And you believe that the Interstellar Government planted the mega-bomb?'

Jake nodded. 'I was called away from the city before the explosion, but only because Admiral Vantard wanted to capture me alive. There was a blinding flash of light and a giant dust cloud. It took me a moment to realise what had happened and then I saw the remains of the city with my own eyes.'

Callidus scowled. 'The Interstellar Government has done some terrible things in the past, but I never dreamt that it was capable of murdering so many innocent people.'

'I'm lucky not to be one of them.'

Jake was surprised to see a tear escape from the fortune seeker's eye and trickle down his cheek.

'I feared you were dead,' said Callidus, wiping his face with his wrist. 'Capio and I saw the explosion on the *Interstellar News* before we lost the stellar-net signal. I had no way of knowing if you were safe.'

'It was the same for me. I was worried that you and Capio had arrived late on Santanova and you had been caught in the blast.'

The two of them walked in silence for a few minutes, savouring the crisp morning air.

'I like your new friend,' said Callidus. 'Kay has guts.'

'That's one way of putting it.' Jake smiled. 'Her heart is in the right place. Granny Leatherhead knew her father, Wild Joe Jagger.'

'I've been meaning to ask you about the Space Dogs,' said Callidus. 'Where are they?'

Jake scooped up some snow and hurled it at the nearest ship. 'Kay reckons that they're being held prisoner aboard the *ISS Magnificent*.'

'What?'

'Apparently, they were arrested while helping the *Divine Wind* to escape. I wish there were a way to rescue them. We could do with a bit more pirate power in our fleet.'

'Agreed,' said Callidus. 'I may not see eye to eye with Granny Leatherhead, so to speak, but we owe that crew a lot, and not just crystals. If it hadn't been for them, neither of us would be standing here today.'

'Yes, but even if we went after the *ISS Magnificent*, how would we break out the Space Dogs?'

'Not easily, but there might be a way. Let me think about it.' Callidus switched to a more casual tone. 'What about your father? Any news?'

Jake told him about Jorge Dasch.

'I know he tried to kill me, but I'm convinced he was telling the truth about seeing my dad alive. It was like a confession or something. What about you? Did you find what you were searching for?'

'You could say that.' Callidus paused to let two young children run past. 'In fact, I found more than I bargained for. It's why I wanted to talk with you.'

Jake could sense that there was something bothering the fortune seeker. 'You were on your way to see a mining crew, the people who left you at a canteen in the seventh solar system when you lost your memories. Were you an asteroid miner?'

'Not exactly.' Callidus indicated for them to sit down on a large flat rock in the shade of the crater wall. 'Believe it or not, their captain remembered me from all those years ago. It turns out that he's the one who named me.'

'I don't understand,' said Jake. 'What do you mean he named you?'

'There's no easy way to say this, Jake.' Callidus rubbed his hands nervously. 'I'm not Callidus Stone.'

The words took a few moments to sink into Jake's weary mind. It was the last thing that he had expected to hear that morning.

'But if you're not Callidus Stone ... who are you?'

'That is an excellent question. Apparently, I was named after the mining ship's computer, C.A.L.L.I.D.U.S. It stands for "Computing And Logistics Logic In Deep Unchartered Space". My surname was given to me because I was as cold as stone when the crew found me.'

Jake's purple eyes traced the crater floor while he tried to make sense of what he was hearing.

'Cal –' he began, but they were interrupted.

'Come quick,' called Nanoo from a side hatch on the *Star Chaser*. 'Kella awake.'

Chapter 8

The Mystery of Callidus Stone

A cry of pain emanated from deep inside the *Star Chaser*. Jake leapt to his feet and sprinted back to the pleasure cruiser, with Callidus close at his heels. They charged through the side hatch and up to the medical bay, where Kella was writhing about on her bed. The ship's medic attempted to restrain her, but Kella was stronger than she looked. Her bloodshot eyes found Jake in the doorway and she thrust out her hand.

'Crystals,' she rasped.

Jake understood. He took off his gold pendant and passed it to her. Kella pressed the three crystals to her face, as though her life depended on it. The medic stepped away as she became still and closed her eyes.

'Will that work?' whispered Callidus, watching her intently.

'No idea,' said Jake. 'I've never seen anyone heal themselves.'

The crystals glowed beneath Kella's fingers as she moved them across her forehead.

'What we do now?' asked Nanoo.

Jake settled himself on one of the spare beds. 'We wait.'

Callidus frowned. 'But we leave for Libertina today.'

'We can still launch the fleet with Kella on board. If we're lucky, she'll be healed by the time we reach the sixth solar system.'

Nanoo pulled up a seat next to Kella's bed. 'It OK, I watch over her.'

'Perhaps she would be better off staying behind at the monastery,' suggested Callidus.

'No,' wheezed Kella. 'I'm coming with you.'

'Are you sure?' checked Jake.

Kella half opened one eye and glared at him. 'I'm doing this for my sister. If the only way to get Jeyne out of Ur-Hal is to take down the Interstellar Government, I want to help.'

'In that case,' said Jake, hopping off the bed and turning to the medic. 'I would like you to tell the crews to prepare for launch within the hour.'

The medic seemed reluctant to leave his patient, but he nodded obediently and left the room.

'What can I do?' asked Callidus.

'You can finish telling me your story,' said Jake. 'Who are you, Cal?'

Nanoo tilted his head. 'What that mean?'

Callidus fidgeted nervously. 'It might be nothing. Probably just a coincidence.'

'What might?' asked Jake. 'Where did the asteroid miners find you?'

Callidus took a long breath. 'I was discovered in space eleven years ago, floating unconscious near an asteroid field in the seventh solar system. According to the captain, I was badly battered and barely alive when the crew brought me aboard. They patched me up and dropped me at the nearest planet with a handful of coins, but I was still disorientated and suffering from amnesia.'

Jake's mouth fell open. 'But that could mean ...'

Callidus locked eyes with him and nodded. 'I could be Andras Cutler. Jake, I could be your father.'

It seemed too incredible to be true. Jake stared at Callidus, as though expecting to find someone else hiding beneath the surface. Was it possible? Could the ex-naval officer really be his missing father? Had Andras Cutler been searching for himself these last few months? Nanoo muttered something in his own language and Kella found the strength to sit up and swear.

'We don't know anything for certain,' said Callidus. 'It might not have been the same asteroid field.'

Jake had been too young to remember his parents, but he had always assumed that he would recognise his father when the time came, that he would somehow just *know*. Perhaps that was why Callidus had caught his attention on Remota. Was that why Jake had felt compelled to follow him? How could he be sure? If only there had been a photo or painting of Andras Cutler on Altus.

'But we don't even look alike,' said Jake, his brain racing.

'You have same chin,' pointed out Nanoo.

'And I have no idea what my nose looked like before it got broken,' said Callidus. 'Which I'm guessing happened around the same time I lost my memory.'

Jake raked his fingers through his own thick brown hair, which looked similar, except it was much lighter. Was this significant? After all, he knew that his mother had been an albino with ivory-blonde hair. He wondered what colour his own eyes had been, before the cyber-monks had replaced them with purple implants. Why had he never thought to ask Father Pius? Would it have proved anything if they had been blue?

'But we don't sound alike,' said Jake. 'And you don't have an Altian accent.'

'Neither do you,' reasoned Callidus. 'My accent cannot be easily placed. It contains elements from each of the planets that I've visited over the years.'

There seemed to be an answer for everything.

'Isn't it, you know, a bit of a coincidence?' asked Jake. 'My father loses his memory, but somehow finds me anyway.'

'I don't know what to think,' said Callidus. 'If I was … am … Andras Cutler, it would explain why I've been so obsessed with Altus. I dreamt about that planet nearly every night for eleven years. Which, incidently, is how long it took me to find you. As far as I was concerned, you were just another clue to help me locate Altus, but what if it was more than that? I was frightened by how familiar the surface looked. It was exactly as I had imagined it … Exactly.'

Jake recalled how Callidus had often talked about Altus in his sleep. Were there forgotten memories buried inside his subconscious?

'You were on Altus for a month,' said Kella, still massaging her cheeks with the crystals. 'If you were Andras Cutler, the Altian people would have recognised you.'

Callidus held his forehead. 'No one had the chance. I was wearing a skull-shaped helmet when Jake defeated Kear Cutler and then I returned to the *Dark Horse*.'

'But someone must have seen your face,' said Jake. 'What about the farmers who helped us to escape?'

'If anyone saw me, they didn't recognise me, but then it has been eleven years since Andras went missing. He would have looked a lot younger when he left Altus and I doubt that he had a beard or a broken nose.'

Jake felt a cocktail of emotions stir inside him. He wanted to be pleased, but there was still too much doubt in his mind. At that moment, it was hard to think of Callidus as anything other than a good friend.

'What do you reckon?' he asked, tentatively. 'Are you the true ruler of Altus and my dad?'

'I honestly don't know,' said Callidus. 'There's no solid proof either way. When I was in the Interstellar Navy, my commander told me that I was a natural leader ... but the ruler of Altus? ... Responsible for a planet? That's a whole different league. All I know is that I've wanted to protect you from the moment we met on Remota. If I'm not Andras Cutler, who am I?'

'Amicus Kent,' blurted Nanoo.

'I'm sorry?'

'Yes, of course,' said Kella. 'He was Andras Cutler's best friend. If you were Jake's father, Amicus would have definitely recognised you.'

'Good point,' conceded Callidus.

Jake thought about their encounter with the Altian general. 'But he did recognise you!'

'What?' exclaimed Kella and Nanoo together.

'Don't you remember?' said Jake. 'He called out "Cutler" when we first met. But he could have been referring to the person standing next to me, which was you, Cal.'

'That's true,' recalled Callidus. 'When I failed to recognise him, he must have assumed that he was mistaken.'

Kella turned her head on the pillow. 'Unless he really was mistaken and you just look a bit like his old friend.'

'What if Amicus thought that you were pretending not to know either of us and he played along?' wondered Jake. 'Think about it. This is the man who left me at a monastery, because he figured that I would be safer not knowing my true identity.'

Callidus held up his hands. 'Alas, we'll never find out what he was really thinking. All I know for certain is that I was not born with the name Callidus Stone.'

'There is one way to be sure.' Jake glanced at his gold pendant. 'We could return to Altus. After the war, I mean. Kear Cutler would recognise his own brother, however much Andras had changed.'

The hatch door opened.

'Is everything all right, my lord?' asked Captain Swan.

Jake hesitated for a second. 'Yes, fine, we were just talking. Are the ships ready to launch?'

'Nearly, we're only waiting for the *Divine Wind*.'

Jake understood the problem.

'Kay,' he sighed.

In his heart, Jake wanted to keep talking with Callidus, but there wasn't much else they could say until they had some proof. The truth would have to wait, they had a war to fight.

The snow on the crater surface was now spoiled as Jake marched over to the *Divine Wind*. His breath escaped from his nostrils in puffs of smoke, like an old steam engine. He would not miss the cold air or the damp in his shoes when they left Shan-Ti. Away from the *Star Chaser*, his mind kept turning to Callidus. Would it be so bad if the fortune seeker was the one person who Jake wanted to find the most? Callidus was his friend after all. But was that enough?

Jake had no idea what his father looked like, so why was he expecting more? In his mind, a faceless image of a strong and heroic Altian leader stood before his people. Jake had spent years dreaming about the day he would find his father, which had been perfect in every detail. Perhaps he felt cheated out of a grand reunion.

'Now is not the time,' he muttered to himself. 'Keep focused.'

A group of colonists and cyber-monks were busy working on the *Divine Wind*. The fire-damaged hull didn't look so bad in the light of day and they had already replaced the broken windows. All that the old star frigate needed now was a lick of paint and a new crew. Jake spotted Kay sitting cross-legged on the loading ramp with her arms folded.

'Good morning,' he said brightly.

'Is it?' she huffed.

'Listen, Kay, I'm sorry that we couldn't go after the Luna Ticks last night, but I have to think of the other vessels. The fleet is almost ready for launch and I want the *Divine Wind* to be our flagship.'

Kay eyed him suspiciously. 'This ship isn't going anywhere without a crew. I'll have to stay behind on my own. No shipmates. No family. No friends.'

'We're your friends,' said Jake. 'And we're not leaving you behind. I can fly the ship, while you watch the scanners. Nanoo can look after the engine and Kella can be the ship's medic.'

'What about gunners?'

'Callidus and Capio can fire the laser cannon.'

Kay unfolded her arms. 'Are you really my friend?'

'Yes, you chumpty,' he laughed. 'Now get this ship ready for launch.'

'Aye, my lord,' she said, springing to her feet.

Jake watched Kay skip up the loading ramp. He had never met anyone as unpredictable as her, but he knew that she could be trusted in battle. There was no doubt in his mind that she would fight by his side until the bitter end.

As he turned to leave, Jake caught sight of Father Benedict walking towards them with two cyber-monks and a large box. Kay paused at the top of the ramp and scratched her eyepatch.

'Good morning,' called out the cyber-abbot.

'I was just on my way to see you,' said Jake.

'To tell me that you're going?'

'I'm afraid it's time.' Jake pointed to the box. 'What's that?'

'It's a leaving present,' said Father Benedict. 'A new eye for Miss Jagger.'

Jake glanced up at Kay. 'Hey, that's magnifty.'

'It's not as sophisticated as your eye implants,' warned Father Benedict. 'We didn't have enough time to produce something that small and complex, but we have been able to rig up a robotic eye that should do the trick.'

Kay looked apprehensively at the box, as though it might contain something grim or dangerous, like a baby kalmar.

'I suppose we had better get on with it,' she said, entering the ship. 'If we're going to launch on time.'

The two cyber-monks followed Kay inside to install the robotic eye. Father Benedict stayed behind to talk with Jake.

'So, this is it,' he said. 'You're off to war.'

'You should come with us,' suggested Jake. 'We could do with some technical support.'

Father Benedict held up his hand. 'I'm sorry, but I never did find my space legs. In fact, I get space sick just thinking about zero gravity.'

'That's OK,' said Jake. 'You've already done plenty.'

'I wish there was more I could do, other than hand out water and broadcast messages.'

'Hey, maybe there is something.' Jake felt a rush of inspiration. 'You can be our eyes and ears.'

Father Benedict frowned. 'You've lost me.'

'Until the stellar-net is back up, we'll only be able to contact passing ships with our short-range communicators,' explained Jake. 'We won't know the Interstellar Navy is coming until they appear on our scanners. But you could use your satellites to keep track of the enemy, while sending us messages to let us know what's happening.'

'You mean like a pirate radio?' mused the cyber-abbot. 'We'll need to hack some satellites in the seventh solar system and work out a way to encrypt the messages, but I suppose it's possible.'

'Does that mean you'll do it?'

Father Benedict stood to attention and saluted. 'Aye, my lord.'

'Good,' said Jake. 'You have less than an hour to set it up.'

'An hour? There's never a dull moment when you're around, is there!' Father Benedict turned to head back to the monastery, when a bloodcurdling scream pierced the air. The cyber-abbot stopped and grimaced at the *Divine Wind*. 'It sounds as though the brothers have removed the faulty eye.'

Chapter 9

Radio Interference

Within the hour, Jake was dressed in his Altian uniform and giving the passenger ships a final inspection. The thick material was uncomfortable and his golden cutlass was heavy, but it wasn't every day that he got to launch a brand new fleet and he wanted to look his best. If nothing else, his appearance might help to inspire the crews as they set off to war. Underneath his jacket, he was wearing the laserproof vest that Nanoo had made him, which had already saved his life once.

Jake paused outside the *Star Chaser* to speak with Captain Swan. 'Are you ready to save the galaxy?'

'Aye, my lord,' said the captain. 'The crew is somewhat nervous, but we're as ready as we'll ever be. I'm sorry that I ever doubted you.'

'No apology necessary,' said Jake. 'If it wasn't for you and your crew, I would not have escaped from Santanova.'

Callidus and Capio appeared, carrying crates of food. Jake tensed at the sight of the fortune seeker, uncertain how he should feel.

'Greetings, my lord,' said Callidus, with a courteous nod.

'Where did you get all that?' asked Jake.

'Father Benedict insisted,' said Capio. 'Not bad, eh? He's even packed some of that tasty stew. Those cyber-monks are so much nicer than space pirates.'

Callidus hoisted his crate on to his shoulder. 'Kay mentioned that you want us aboard the *Divine Wind* with you.'

'Is that OK?' asked Jake.

Callidus smiled. 'I can't think of anywhere else I would rather be.'

'Thank you …' Jake hesitated and lowered his voice. 'What do I call you now?'

Callidus was so surprised by this question, he nearly dropped his crate. 'Cal is fine, until we know who I am for sure.'

Jake finished the inspection and headed to the monastery, where the cyber-monks and novices had lined up to say goodbye. Father Benedict stood at the front in his flapping robes, like a big black vulture, next to a woman in a pastel green suit.

'Deputy prime minister,' said Jake. 'What brings you here?'

'Actually, I'm the prime minister now,' corrected Kristina Lemark, with the faintest of smiles. 'It was made official last night. I came to thank you and wish you luck, Mr Cutler. Despite what I said the other day, what you're doing is truly daring and noble. I hope it makes a difference.'

'Thank you, prime minister. I'll make good use of your warships.'

Father Benedict shook his hand. 'Take care, Jake. I'll do my best to guide you in the right direction.'

'Thanks, father, I look forward to your first broadcast.'

With a final wave, Jake returned to the *Divine Wind*, which would be the first ship to launch. Nanoo had already checked its engine and he was now helping Kella into the medical bay, where she would finish healing herself. Callidus and Capio were stationed on the gun deck, where Nanoo had installed two new laser cannon, alongside the old pink weapons.

Kay was resting in her quarters, following her robotic eye transplant. According to Father Benedict, the operation had been a success, but it would take a few hours for the swelling to go down; therefore Jake would have to launch the freshly painted star frigate on his own. It was comforting to have his friends around him as the fleet left for war. But at the same time, it meant that the people he cared about most were aboard the same ship. If anything happened to the *Divine Wind*, they would all be lost.

Jake knew that some people would find it strange that he wanted to pilot a space pirate ship, when he could command any vessel in the fleet. But Jake wasn't like other leaders: he was a thirteen-year-old spacejacker and he was proud of it. The fact that he'd grown up studying technology instead of politics didn't matter. It was what he did now that counted. Jake was going to fight the galactic war his way and the *Divine Wind* was the perfect ship for a pirate prince.

With a smile to himself, he started to sing the first space shanty that the Space Dogs had ever taught him:

'Take me to the launch pad, boy,
Load me up and strap me in,
Life among the stars, ahoy,
Proud to be space pirate kin.
Free to roam, away we cast,
Dogs of space will always win,
Never forget times gone past,
Proud to be space pirate kin.'

Jake reached the bridge and strapped himself into the pilot's seat. He glanced momentarily at the empty chair behind him, where Kay would normally sit, before activating the intercom and snatching up the microphone.

'Attention, shipmates,' he said to the crew. 'It's time to strap yourselves in and wave goodbye to Shan-Ti.'

Humming to himself, Jake commenced the launch sequence and the engine fired up. He gripped the controls and focused on the sky above. This was finally it, the moment that the Independent Alliance took to the stars and fought for freedom. Jake could feel its significance course through his body, blended with a mixture of fear and excitement. He released the thrusters and the *Divine Wind* powered forward, bumping across the crater floor and gathering speed. Flecks of snow bombarded the window as the bright yellow hull lifted into the air.

'Watch out, Interstellar Navy,' he shouted, as the star frigate cleared the crater wall and soared into the sky. 'Here comes the Independent Alliance.'

The *Divine Wind* charged through the planet's atmosphere and burst into space, followed by the *Star Chaser* and the ten remaining passenger ships. All of the fighter craft were now tucked neatly into special harnesses on the sides of the bigger vessels, ready for action. Jake swelled with pride at what everyone had achieved in a couple of days. What was once a convoy of refugees seeking sanctuary, was now a fleet of battleworthy ships. He might only be a pirate prince, but at that moment he felt like a king leading his army to war.

As Kristina Lemark had promised, two sleek red warships from the Shan-Ti planetary guard were waiting for them in orbit. These were not as large as the Interstellar Navy warships, but they each carried a squadron of fighters and they bore a dozen laser cannon. Jake activated the communicator.

'Ahoy, Shan-Ti warships. This is Jake Cutler, leader of the Independent Alliance. It's good of you to join us.'

'Ahoy there. This is Captain Angela Harley of the *Scarlet Sabre* at your service.'

'Ahoy, Jake Cutler. This is Captain Lee Quinn of the *Astral Queen* awaiting your orders.'

Jake led the fleet into open space, being careful not to accelerate too fast for the slow passenger ships. As they left Shan-Ti behind, his eyes feasted on the ocean of stars ahead.

'How's my ship?' asked a grumpy voice.

'Kay?' Jake turned in his seat. 'Sorry, I didn't hear –'

Words suddenly failed him and his jaw dropped at the sight of the pirate captain.

'What's the matter?' she asked. 'Do I have something on my face?'

'No,' he said, a little too quickly. 'I mean, yes, of course, but, you know.'

'It's OK, you can say it,' she sighed. 'I look like one of those Hacker Jacker robots.'

If Jake was honest, Kay was far more frightening than the crew of robot space pirates they had met, but he was not about to tell her that. The cyber-monks had installed a rather bulky metal plate over her scars, which contained a crude camera lens surrounded by tiny lights. Her skin was still bruised and tender from the operation, making her appear like a scientific experiment that had gone wrong. For the first time in his life, Jake appreciated his purple eye implants.

'How's your vision?' he asked.

'Not bad,' she said. 'But this thing will take some getting used to before I can shoot straight.'

'The ship is fine. Its hull is holding together and none of the windows have cracked. If you ask me, the enhanced engine is begging to be tested out, but we have to keep pace with the rest of the fleet.'

'Don't worry, I'm sure we'll get a chance to …' Kay's good eye flicked to the front window. 'Watch out!'

Jake had not been watching where they were going. A large chunk of metal flew past the *Divine Wind*, missing it by inches.

'That was close,' he said, before spotting something else floating towards them.

Kay squinted at the window. 'Is that what I think it is?'

Jake felt a growing sense of dread as the object drew nearer. 'It's a dead body.'

Jake slowed the *Divine Wind* to avoid hitting the corpse.

'There's another one,' said Kay, pointing to a patch of nearby space. 'And two more behind it.'

The fleet had entered a field of bodies and debris, which drifted eerily past the window like something out of a nightmare. Jake stared at the gruesome figures, who were frozen in their final poses.

'What happened here?'

'It's a shipwreck,' said Kay.

'Do you think it was spacejacked?' wondered Jake. 'I can't see any survivors.'

'Hey, that was my first mate,' shouted Kay, as a grisly grey face slid past the window. 'It's the Luna Ticks!'

Jake spotted the remains of the stolen passenger ship, which was little more than a jagged metal skeleton now.

'It looks as though someone else got to them first,' he said.

Kay turned pale. 'That was my crew … They were in our best ship. Who would do such a thing?'

The communicator speaker crackled.

'Ahoy, *Divine Wind*,' said Captain Swan. 'Are there any survivors?'

'Ahoy, *Star Chaser*.' Jake scanned the space around them. 'It doesn't look like it and the *Titanicus* is a wreck. I doubt that we'll find anything worth salvaging.'

'In that case, let's keep moving,' said Captain Swan. 'Father Benedict, I don't know if you're listening, but we could do with some guidance. The *Titanicus* has been destroyed. Are we in danger?'

There was silence, except for the hum of space static.

'Father Benedict?' echoed Jake.

'Ahoy there, Independent Alliance,' said the cyber-abbot cheerily. 'This is Radio Interference with its first broadcast. We've just picked up a naval communication. It looks as though the Luna Ticks ran into Admiral Vantard as they fled from Shan-Ti, but you're in no immediate danger, because the *ISS Magnificent* has set course for the Tego Nebula in the seventh solar system. The only other vessel near you is a naval gunship called the *ISS Timidus*, which is patrolling the edge of the fifth solar system.'

'The *ISS Magnificent*.' Jake turned to Kay. 'That's where the Space Dogs are being held.'

'What's it doing here, in the fourth solar system?' she wondered.

'Admiral Vantard was supposed to arrest me on Santanova after the gathering. It sounds as though he's heading to the seventh solar system to help with the attack. This could be our only chance to save Granny Leatherhead and the others.'

'How's the fleet supposed to catch the *ISS Magnificent*? It might be heading the same way as us, but there's no way that our passenger ships can match its speed.'

Callidus and Capio entered the bridge.

'Did you hear?' asked Jake. 'The *ISS Magnificent* is about to leave this solar system.'

'We heard,' said Callidus. 'Are we going after it?'

Jake shook his head. 'The fleet is too slow.'

'But the *Divine Wind* might be able to catch it,' said Kay, with a glint in her eye. 'If we leave the others behind.'

'Go after the *ISS Magnificent* on our own? Are you crazy?' asked Capio. 'Actually, no need to answer that. But Jake is the leader of the Independent Alliance. He can't leave the fleet.'

'Capio has a point,' said Jake. 'Although, I could ask Captain Swan to take charge until I get back. How long would we be gone?'

'It would take us a few hours to reach the *ISS Magnificent*,' estimated Kay. 'But it might take a while to disable their engines and free the Space Dogs.'

'Two laser cannon against a naval warship?' Callidus whistled. 'I'm afraid that even with Nanoo's modifications, we wouldn't survive a direct attack. Perhaps this requires a more subtle approach.'

'I'm not painting my ship midnight blue,' protested Kay, her robotic eye moving in random directions.

'There's not enough time to disguise the *Divine Wind*,' said Callidus. 'But there might be another way.'

Capio groaned. 'Here we go again.'

Captain Wortus had his orders. The *ISS Timidus* was to scour the fifth solar system in search of the teenage space pirate, Kid Cutler. Wortus was determined to capture the boy personally, because he had a score to settle. A few weeks ago, the purple-eyed punk had ambushed his crew and used their gunship's computer to access the main naval server. Wortus was lucky not to have been court-martialled. At least his ship had been spared.

The *ISS Timidus* was now docked at a squalid excuse of a trading station. Captain Wortus wanted to question the traders about Kid Cutler, while his troopers searched the place for stolen goods and illegal weapons.

By the time Wortus reached the main concourse, flanked by his troopers, the traders were already gathered and waiting for him. He took one look at their cheap clothes and snorted in disgust.

'What is it with you people and these ridiculous wide-brimmed hats?' he sneered, taking one from a trader's head and examining it. 'Are you worried it might rain in space?'

Captain Wortus tossed the hat over his shoulder and moved along the line to the next trader, whose milky-white eyes stared into empty space beneath clumps of grey hair. At her feet, a scruffy brown dog barked at him.

'Do you have a licence to keep pets aboard this trading station?' he asked abruptly.

'No,' said the trader nervously. 'I'm blind and this dog guides me.'

'A likely story. All of the blind people I know use house robots, not flea-ridden mongrels. We'll have to confiscate this animal under Interstellar Law.'

'But I can't afford a house robot,' she protested.

The dog barked more ferociously.

'Will someone shut this ruddy mutt up,' snapped Captain Wortus, kicking the dog with the side of his gravity boot.

'You shouldn't have done that,' said the next trader, producing a golden cutlass from inside his coat.

Captain Wortus froze as the tip of the blade pressed into his stomach. He had a pretty good idea who was at the other end of the sword, because it was not the first time that this had happened. He caught sight of two purple eyes blazing beneath a wide-brimmed hat.

'Oh no,' he whimpered. 'Not again.'

'Nobody move,' shouted Jake, throwing off his disguise. 'Drop your weapons or I'll run this wretch-ard through.'

A few of the troopers looked tempted to take the risk, but then several traders stepped forward, bran-dishing old pistols, swords, clubs and a growling dog.

The naval troopers put down their plasma rifles and surrendered.

'What do you want?' moaned Captain Wortus. 'Are you after more information?'

Jake smirked. 'No, this time we want your ship.'

Chapter 10

The Belly of the Beast

The *ISS Timidus* cruised through the stars with Jake at the helm and Callidus on the scanners. It had been several hours since the naval gunship had left the trading station and it had almost caught up with the *ISS Magnificent*. Kay had been reluctant to leave the *Divine Wind* behind, but the traders had promised to keep the star frigate safe. Jake was feeling daring and rebellious after spacejacking a naval vessel. It was also nice to be chasing after Admiral Vantard for a change, instead of the other way around.

Captain Swan had strongly objected to the *Divine Wind* leaving on its own without an escort. Jake had said that he was only scouting ahead and the fleet should continue without him. This was fine, as long as Father Benedict didn't broadcast the truth, because it was unlikely that the other captains would understand why Jake was risking the mission for a crew of spacejackers. If all went well, he would be back before the fleet reached the next solar system. But if not, he was confident that Captain Swan would stick to the plan and go to war without him.

Was the risk worth taking? If Jake was honest, he couldn't stand the thought of the Space Dogs suffering. But it was more than that: the Independent Alliance needed fast ships and crews with battle experience. Just the sight of the *Dark Horse* would spread panic throughout the naval fleet, because the naval troops believed that the old cargo hauler was responsible for destroying the *ISS Colossus*.

'What is plan?' asked Nanoo, who was strapped into one of the gunners' seats.

'It's simple,' said Callidus. 'We use the *ISS Timidus* to dock inside the *ISS Magnificent* and then we locate the Space Dogs.'

'Won't someone notice a group of strangers wandering around?' Kella still looked red and sore, but she had insisted on joining them.

'Not if we're disguised in naval uniforms,' said Jake. 'I found a stack of them in a locker at the rear and we already have plasma rifles.'

'Do naval troopers normally have pink curls?' asked Kay, holding out a strand of her hair.

'No,' said Callidus. 'Nor do they have lilac skin or report for duty with severe burns.'

'And I expect they don't have purple eyes either,' pointed out Kella.

'I'll be fine,' said Jake. 'But I have a different job for you three.'

Kay frowned at him. 'It had better be dangerous.'

Jake smiled mischievously. 'I need you to set some explosives and steal back the *Dark Horse*. Does that sound dangerous enough?'

Kay beamed. 'Aye, my lord.'

Jake, Callidus and Capio changed into the midnight blue uniforms. It was no surprise that the smallest was still too large for Jake. He had to fold back the shirt cuffs and stuff the trouser legs into his gravity boots. At least there was a matching cap with a low peak that he could pull over his eyes. Capio squeezed into his uniform, but he had to hold his breath to do up the shirt and trousers. Jake found it disturbing how well the clothes fitted Callidus, who looked tall and handsome as a naval officer.

'It has been a while since I wore one of these,' said Callidus, fingering the collar. 'When I was in the Interstellar Navy, my first assignment was aboard one of these gunships. Mind you, they have changed a bit over the years. I can stand up now without banging my head.'

Jake checked the *ISS Magnificent* on the scanner. 'Won't we need a password or something to dock?'

'Good point.' Callidus activated the communicator and adjusted the settings to a secret frequency that he knew the cyber-monks would be monitoring. 'This is a special request for Radio Interference. If you can hear us, father, we're aboard a naval gunship and we need the latest security codes to access a naval warship.'

Within a few minutes, the *ISS Timidus* received a message from Father Benedict with the code that Callidus had requested.

'Impressive,' marvelled Capio. 'Is there anything those cyber-monks can't do?'

'They know more about technology than anyone in the galaxy,' said Jake. 'It was the cyber-monks who invented the stellar-net.'

The *ISS Magnificent* was now visible through the front window. Jake could make out the United Worlds flag on its heavily armoured hull. He stared resentfully at the circle of seven blue stars on a white background. The flag had once been a symbol of order and unity, but it had become tainted by the warmongering Interstellar Government.

Callidus signalled for everyone to be quiet as he activated the communicator.

'Ahoy, *ISS Magnificent*,' he said, briskly. 'This is naval gunship *ISS Timidus* requesting permission to dock and refuel.'

There was a brief silence before someone replied with a crisp first solar system accent. 'Ahoy, *ISS Timidus*, this is the ship-based dock master, we've got you on our scanners and we've confirmed your registration plates. Do you have the security code?'

'Affirmative,' said Callidus. 'Starlight-four-nine-seven-comet.'

Jake held his breath as they waited for the response.

'Security code confirmed,' said the voice. 'Please proceed to launch lock two and wait for the green light.'

'Thank you, dock master.' Callidus switched off the communicator and smiled. 'There's no going back now.'

Jake flew the *ISS Timidus* alongside the *ISS Magnificent* and spotted a huge launch lock with the number two painted on it. He waited for the doors to open and the light above them to turn green. It was strange to be this close to a naval warship without the sound of laser cannon fire. His eyes scanned its mighty gun ports and midnight blue hull with a mixture of fascination and fear. It made him realise the sheer scale of the challenge ahead. His collection of customised passenger ships would have to defeat a whole fleet of these metal monsters.

The launch lock doors finished opening to reveal a cavernous chamber and the light flashed green.

'Here we go,' said Jake, pulling the controls. 'Into the belly of the beast.'

The *ISS Timidus* swooped towards the opening.

'Steady now,' warned Callidus. 'There isn't much room inside that launch lock, so you'll need to enter it slowly and be ready with your landing gear.'

Jake eased off the thrusters and lined up the gunship. His landing had to be good, otherwise it might draw attention.

'You're too far to the left,' said Kay.

'No, he's not,' argued Callidus. 'But he does need to lift the nose.'

'Never mind the nose,' said Capio. 'It's the tail that he has to watch.'

'Do you mind?' snapped Jake. 'This is hard enough without you backseat pilots distracting me.'

The others fell silent as the *ISS Timidus* passed through the huge doors and set down in the centre of the launch lock. Jake activated the breaks and let go of the controls. The outer doors clamped shut, sealing them inside the chamber.

'Good work,' said Callidus. 'That was even better than your crater landing.'

Jake smiled. 'Yeah, well you know what they say about practice.'

Callidus nudged Capio. 'Now comes the difficult bit.'

The inner doors parted to reveal an enormous hangar deck full of naval shuttles and fighter craft. There were even a couple of chubby Gork fighters docked near the launch lock. Pilots and mechanics worked on their ships in a hive of activity, while chunky maintenance droids trundled back and forth with spare parts. The idea of finding the Space Dogs had seemed so simple back on the *Divine Wind*, but now Jake realised the immensity of their challenge. How in the name of Zerost would they locate a handful of prisoners inside such a vast ship?

Jake steered the *ISS Timidus* out of the launch lock and parked it neatly alongside the two Gork fighters. As he turned off the engine, a maintenance droid appeared with a trolley of fuel cells. Jake scanned the rows of naval craft and located what he was looking for. His most favourite vessel in the whole galaxy was docked near the opposite wall, a plump old cargo hauler named the *Dark Horse*. His heart leapt at the sight of the disguised pirate ship and he longed to be aboard it.

Callidus located a large crate of explosives inside the gunship, which he handed to Kay, Kella and Nanoo. 'When the alarm sounds, it will mean that we've released the Space Dogs. The moment you hear it, I want you to set the timer on the explosives for ten minutes and then get yourselves aboard the *Dark Horse*. If we're not back by the time the *ISS Timidus* blows, it will mean that we've been caught and you should leave without us.'

'But –' began Kay.

'No arguments,' said Callidus. 'It's standard naval procedure to open the launch locks when there's a serious explosion or fire. The loss of oxygen will choke the flames, in the same way that Jake used space to put out the fire on the *Divine Wind*. This will be your only chance to escape.'

'But none of us can fly,' protested Kay.

Callidus picked up a naval pilot's manual and tossed it to Nanoo, who caught the heavy document.

'Nanoo is a smart lad,' said Callidus. 'If we don't make it back in time, I'm sure that he'll be able to work out the controls, so you can find the fleet.'

'Will ten minutes be enough time for you to get back?' asked Kella.

'It will have to be,' said Jake. 'Because we can't afford to hang about once Admiral Vantard knows we're aboard.'

'Don't worry,' assured Callidus. 'I know my way around a naval warship. We'll be fine, as long as we keep our heads.'

Jake stood up and pulled on his cap.

'Let's do it.'

Callidus led Jake and Capio out of the rear hatch and on to the rutted hangar deck floor. The air was alive with the sound of machinery, robots and human voices, which clashed noisily with the hum of the warship engine.

Jake had left his golden cutlass behind with Kay, because it would have been too conspicuous. Instead, he and Capio carried plasma rifles over their shoulders and naval swords in their belts. Callidus was dressed as an officer and was therefore armed with a laser pistol.

'Good luck,' whispered Kay, closing the door behind them.

'You too,' mouthed Jake through the rear porthole window.

There were several ways to enter and exit the hangar deck. The three of them walked calmly over to a circular hatch on the far wall. Callidus opened it and they filed into a bright and spacious corridor, which looked similar to those of the *ISS Colossus* super-destroyer.

Jake felt strange to be back aboard a naval warship, as though he were revisiting a bad dream. He half expected to see the sour face of Admiral Algor Nex or glittering make-up of Commissioner Lamia Dolosa from the Galactic Trade Corporation.

'In here,' said Callidus, entering a maintenance lift. 'It will take us up to the droid charging station, directly below the main prison level. But we had better hold on, because this lift is not designed for humans.'

Jake and Capio squeezed into the narrow compartment with Callidus. The doors closed and Jake braced himself. But nothing could have prepared him for how fast the lift moved. Without warning, it shot upwards at the speed of a laser bolt, leaving Jake's stomach behind. His legs buckled under the acceleration and he found himself sliding down the wall. It was like being squashed by an invisible kalmar.

Just as Capio turned white, the lift came to an abrupt halt, hurling its passengers into the air. Jake banged his head on the compartment ceiling before returning to the floor with a bump. The door opened and the three of them spilled out on to a dimly lit walkway lined with droids.

'Can they see us?' asked Jake.

'No, they're recharging their batteries,' said Callidus. 'Just ignore them and follow me, but try not to make any noise.'

Jake hurried along the walkway behind the others, keeping his eyes on the inactive droids.

Crash!

Jake jumped in surprise and looked around for their attacker, but none of the droids had moved. In front of him, Capio stood frozen, while a canister of machine grease rolled noisily at his feet.

'Watch it, you idiot,' hissed Callidus. 'If you wake them up, we'll have to explain what we're doing here.'

The three of them hastened along the walkway, their gravity boots gently clipping the metal floor, but the damage had already been done. Several lights blinked on the nearest droids, while wall panels beeped and cables unplugged.

'Hurry up,' urged Jake.

Callidus reached a small hatch at the end of the walkway and flung it open, providing access to a narrow shaft. Capio threw himself inside and started to climb the thin ladder, while Callidus stood guard with his laser pistol drawn. Jake entered the hatch and glanced over his shoulder to see a huddle of droids rolling towards them. He quickly clambered up the ladder after Capio, as Callidus stepped inside and sealed the hatch behind them.

'Do you think they'll report us?' asked Jake.

'Let's hope not,' said Callidus. 'Maintenance droids are curious, but not very bright. I doubt that they got a good look at us.'

'How high do we have to climb?' panted Capio.

'Stop at the next hatch,' instructed Callidus. 'But try not to make any noise this time.'

Jake peered down the shaft, expecting to see the hatch pop open at any moment. He was pretty sure that maintenance droids couldn't climb ladders, but he didn't want to find out.

Capio reached the next level and stopped. 'Now what?'

'When you step through that hatch, act as though it's the most natural thing in the universe,' said Callidus. 'I used to take shortcuts through maintenance shafts when I was a naval officer and no one ever challenged me.'

Capio nodded and opened the hatch, flooding the shaft with bright light. One by one, they stepped out into an empty corridor. To their left were the main crew lifts and to their right was the entrance to the prison block. Jake peered at the secure-looking door, which seemed impenetrable.

'Cal, are you sure about this?'

Callidus closed the hatch with an odd, stony expression. 'We'll get you inside, no problem. It's getting out that will be difficult.'

'No kidding,' said Jake. 'We had better hurry. What's our next move?'

Callidus raised his laser pistol. 'Jake Cutler, I'm arresting you for crimes against the United Worlds.'

Chapter 11

The Unturned Stone

Jake stared wordlessly down the barrel of the laser pistol, while Capio confiscated his plasma rifle and sword.

'I had better hold on to these,' said the stocky man.

Callidus unclipped a set of handcuffs from his belt and tossed them to Jake, who caught them and placed them on his wrists. He was then marched at gunpoint to the prison entrance, where Callidus banged on the door with his fist. A display screen activated on the corridor wall, revealing the bald head and bullish face of a prison guard.

'Yes?' he said, squinting at the camera. 'Who's there? I'm not expecting anyone.'

'Open the door,' commanded Callidus. 'This is Captain Stone of the *ISS Timidus* with a code four prisoner.'

The guard noticed the officer's uniform and hastened to let them inside.

'A code four?' he said, as they entered. 'Who is it?'

Callidus pulled off Jake's cap and pushed him forward. 'We've arrested the wanted space pirate, Jake Cutler. We caught him impersonating a naval trooper.'

The guard's face lit up at the sight of Jake's purple eyes and thick brown hair.

'Kid Cutler,' he sneered. 'Not so scary now, sunshine.'

'You won't get away with this,' growled Jake. 'I'll destroy this ship. Do you hear me?'

Callidus laughed. 'Let's put him in the same cell as his crew of Space Dogs. Admiral Vantard wants to question them personally.'

'Aye, captain.' The guard tightened Jake's handcuffs and gripped his arm. 'We can always find room for one more spacejacker.'

Jake was hauled past a series of numbered doors, while Callidus and Capio followed behind.

'Let me go,' he shouted.

'Here we are,' said the guard, stopping at door twelve. 'Your new home.'

Jake pulled at the handcuffs. 'You can't do this to me.'

The guard ignored him and pressed an intercom button on the wall. 'All prisoners move away from the door.'

After checking that Callidus and Capio had their guns at the ready, the guard tapped a sequence of digits on a control panel. The door opened to reveal a narrow cell containing eight people, who cowered against the far wall. Their faces were so bloodied and bruised, it took Jake a moment to recognise his old crew.

'What have you done to them?' he snarled.

The guard laughed nastily. 'It's not them you should be worried about.'

'Is that so?' Jake stood in the cell doorway, the handcuffs biting into his wrists and his heart pounding with anger at the sight of his wounded friends.

'What are you waiting for?' asked the guard. 'We can do this the hard way if you prefer?'

'Oh, I don't think that'll be necessary,' said Callidus, turning his laser pistol on the guard. 'But thank you for opening the door.'

'Hey, what's going on?' spluttered the bald man.

Capio took the handcuffs off Jake and instead placed them on the guard.

'I'm afraid it's a double-cross,' said Jake, rubbing his wrists. 'You've just let three imposters into your prison block, not one.'

The guard swore out loud and attempted to run away, but Capio tackled him to the ground. He thrashed about on the grated floor, like a fish out of water, until Callidus prodded him with the laser pistol.

'I hate to interrupt,' croaked a familiar voice, 'but what in the name of Zerost are you lot doing aboard the *ISS Magnificent*?'

Granny Leatherhead stood in the doorway, propped up by her master-at-arms, Kodan. Jake was relieved to see the tough old captain of the *Dark Horse*, but she showed clear signs of maximum interrogation. Her long silver hair hung in straggles around her hooked nose and her face was badly bruised beneath her crusty leather eyepatch.

'We're here to rescue you,' he said. 'But we need to move fast.'

The crew winced in pain as they hobbled out of the cell. Jake checked that no one was missing. After the captain and Kodan limped the first mate, Farid. He was followed by the blue-haired pilot, Nichelle, whose skin bore fresh whip marks. Woorak, a muscular gunner with thick dreadlocks, supported his gnarly-looking shipmate, Maaka 'Metal Head', who seemed barely conscious. At the rear, the chief engineer, Scargus, was held up by his assistant, Manik the mechanic. The only member of the crew missing was Squawk, the ship's parrot.

'How will we get them back to the hangar deck?' asked Capio.

Now that they had found the Space Dogs, it was obvious that the crew was in no condition to climb ladders or ride robot lifts.

'We'll have to find another way back,' said Jake.

Woorak grabbed hold of the terrified guard and pushed him into the empty cell.

'Let's s-s-see how y-y-you like it,' he stuttered, closing the door and scrambling the code.

Callidus handed Jake back his cap and weapons. 'I had hoped to avoid the main crew lifts, but it doesn't seem as though we have much choice now.'

Jake helped to carry Scargus to the lift doors.

'Hello there, Jakey-boy,' wheezed the old pirate. 'How was the speech?'

'My speech?' said Jake in surprise. 'Don't you know?'

'Know what?' croaked Granny Leatherhead.

Jake told them about the mega-bomb on Santanova.

'Now I'm leading a fleet of independent colony ships to the seventh solar system to stop the Interstellar Navy,' he said. 'Before we fight our way to Domus in the first to take down the Interstellar Government. We're called the Independent Alliance.'

'Grubber me, lad!' exclaimed Granny Leatherhead. 'We let you out of our sight for a couple of weeks and this is what happens. Are you addicted to trouble?'

'Perhaps,' said Jake. 'But someone has to make a stand.'

'What's the plan?' asked Farid, as they reached the lifts.

'We head for the hangar deck and hope for the best,' said Callidus, pressing the button. 'I'm not going to lie to you, this could get tricky.'

The lift seemed to take forever and Jake knew that the alarm might sound at any moment. Would ten minutes be enough time to get everyone back to the *Dark Horse*? The lift arrived and Jake pulled his cap lower over his eyes. Inside the compartment were two naval troopers and a fighter pilot. All of them looked startled to see the rabble of roughed-up prisoners.

'It's OK, we'll wait for the next lift,' said Callidus. 'We're taking these space pirates back for maximum interrogation.'

The doors closed and the lift disappeared. It was another agonising minute before the next one arrived, but this time it was empty.

'Where's Squawk?' asked Jake, as he herded the crew inside the compartment.

'He's hiding aboard the *Dark Horse*,' said Manik. 'When we were captured, I left him in the engine room with some water and a bag of bird seed.'

The lift was slower than the one used by maintenance droids. It stopped twice on its way to the hangar deck, but there was no room inside for any other passengers.

'Keep your nerve, Jake,' whispered Callidus. 'If we're lucky, we'll get back to the ship before Admiral Vantard discovers that something is wrong.'

As soon as these words left his mouth, a shrill alarm pierced the air.

'The prison guard,' guessed Capio. 'Someone must have found him.'

Callidus checked his wrist computer. 'Our ten minutes start now.'

'Ten minutes until what?' asked Maaka, squinting through swollen eyes.

'We have a deadline,' said Jake. 'And it's not one we want to miss.'

After what seemed like an age, the lift stopped and the doors opened. Callidus led the injured pirate crew into the corridor and towards the main hangar deck entrance. The Space Dogs did their best to hurry, but they were frustratingly slow.

Callidus kept checking his wrist computer and muttering to himself. 'There's still time.'

The alarm seemed to grow louder as they neared the hangar deck.

'Keep going,' said Jake. 'We're almost there.'

The entrance door opened and three figures marched into the corridor, deep in conversation. It took a moment for them to realise that they were not alone. All three of them stopped in their tracks and stared at the escaping prisoners.

It might have been comical, if the situation hadn't been so serious.

The first person was a handsome man, with fine copper hair and a bottle green uniform. Jake recognised him immediately from the *Interstellar News*. It was Admiral Vantard. As their eyes met, it was difficult to know who was more surprised.

'Kid Cutler,' said the admiral theatrically.

The other two people – a man and a woman – looked positively alarmed. Jake guessed by their sparkling suits and matching diamond brooches that they were representatives from the Galactic Trade Corporation.

'That's right,' said Jake, stepping in front of his injured shipmates. 'I've come for the Space Dogs.'

Admiral Vantard snorted. 'Over my dead body.'

Jake placed a hand on the hilt of his sword. 'Whatever it takes to protect my people.'

In a flash, Admiral Vantard reached for his chrome laser pistol and drew it, but Jake was faster. He unsheathed his sword and swung the blade upwards, catching the pistol and knocking it out of the admiral's hand. His naval sword was lighter than the golden cutlass and it responded well. Admiral Vantard cursed and unsheathed his own sword, a bronze-handled sabre with two slender blades carved from bone.

'Seal the entrance,' barked Admiral Vantard to the man from the Galactic Trade Corporation. 'No one is leaving.'

The admiral lunged at Jake, who raised his blade to block the attack, but he was restricted by the plasma rifle strapped to his back. Jake spun on the spot and let the barrel of the gun take the hit, before turning back to counterstrike. As he ducked and weaved, it became clear that the admiral was a skilled swordfighter.

'Get out of the way,' shouted Callidus, his laser pistol raised. 'So I can get a clear shot.'

But it was too late. The man from the Galactic Trade Corporation had retreated back inside the hangar deck and locked the door, leaving them trapped in the corridor. His colleague had been too slow and she cowered behind Admiral Vantard.

'Get the others to the ship,' said Jake, using the plasma rifle to block another hit. 'Find another entrance. I'll give you a head start and then follow behind.'

'We're not leaving without you,' protested Callidus.

Jake had no time to argue. 'That's a direct order, Cal.'

The fortune seeker hesitated for a second, apparently torn with indecision, but then he checked his wrist computer. 'Aye, my lord. Just don't be long.'

'Go!' cried Jake, as the double-bladed bone sword ripped the shoulder of his naval uniform.

Callidus and Capio led the Space Dogs around a corner and out of sight. Jake wondered how long to leave it before he chased after them.

'That was very noble of you,' mocked Admiral Vantard.

'Not all spacejackers are the same,' said Jake, using an attack that Scargus had taught him, which involved a feint to the left, before slicing his blade to the right.

Admiral Vantard deflected the blow. 'No, some of them like to start wars.'

Jake raised his sword, ready to fend off the counter-attack, but his arm was beginning to tire. 'We both know who planted the mega-bomb on Santanova.'

'What's this?' Admiral Vantard paused in mid-strike. 'More lies?'

'Never trust a space pirate,' hissed the woman from the Galactic Trade Corporation, who had flattened herself up against the locked door.

'Trust?' said Jake, angrily. 'I'm not the one attacking independent colonies.'

Admiral Vantard raised his sword. 'As you say, whatever it takes to protect my people.'

The admiral's eyes darted to the fallen laser pistol. Jake used the distraction to his advantage. He sunk his blade deep into the admiral's leg and felt it cut through flesh. Vantard cried out in pain and punched Jake in the face with the hand guard of his sabre. The engraved metal surface felt like a hover-tank as it connected with Jake's cheek. He let go of his sword and staggered backwards, his vision obscured by a shower of bright lights. In front of him, he heard movement as his blade slipped from his hand and clattered to the floor.

He was blind and unarmed.

Chapter 12

The Countdown

Jake swayed on the spot, his vision swimming with static.

'Get the laser pistol,' shouted Admiral Vantard.

There was a frantic scrabbling and Jake knew that he had only seconds before the woman picked up the fallen weapon. He slid the plasma rifle from his back and blinked rapidly as he fumbled for the trigger. His fingers closed around the hand grip and he held up the rifle.

'No one move,' he warned, his vision starting to clear.

In front of him, he could make out the representative from the Galactic Trade Corporation sprawled across the floor, her hand inches from the chrome laser pistol. Jake kicked it out of her reach and indicated for her to join Admiral Vantard, who was propped up against the corridor wall, holding his blood-soaked leg with one hand and his macabre sabre with the other.

'Space pirate scum,' spat the woman viciously.

Jake had never fired a plasma rifle, but he was not about to try it now. There were several dents in the barrel from the double-bladed bone sword, which might cause the weapon to misfire. He needed to leave, before Admiral Vantard realised that something was wrong. Jake had given the others a good head start and there could only be a few minutes left before the *ISS Timidus* exploded.

'Well?' demanded Admiral Vantard. 'What are you waiting for?'

'He can't do it,' said the woman from the Galactic Trade Corporation, her heavily mascaraed eyes flaring. 'He's scared to pull the trigger. Not so dreadful in the flesh, are you, dear.'

'Lost your nerve, eh?' Admiral Vantard pushed himself away from the wall and raised his sword. 'I'm going to chop you into kalmar bait.'

Jake hastily backed away. There wasn't time for another sword fight, he had to get to the hangar deck. Admiral Vantard limped after him, shouting like a madman, while the woman from the Galactic Trade Corporation made a fresh grab for the laser pistol. Jake threw down the faulty plasma rifle and sprinted up the corridor, as laser bolts seared the wall behind him. He turned the corner into a new section, only to discover a row of identical hatches. Which one had the crew gone through?

Jake could hear Admiral Vantard limping closer. He had to act fast.

'What's that?' he muttered, spotting a cross carved crudely on the middle door.

BOOM!

The corridor shook violently as something exploded nearby, which Jake guessed was the *ISS Timidus*. He steadied himself and waited for the vibrations to stop. Was he too late?

'Attention,' broadcast a placid voice through the corridor speakers. 'All personnel to evacuate the hangar deck immediately. Inner doors will seal in sixty seconds, fifty-nine, fifty-eight ...'

Jake swallowed hard. He had less than a minute to find the others.

'Come back and fight,' shouted Admiral Vantard, hopping into view. 'I've not finished with you, spacejacker.'

Jake opened the marked door and ducked inside a cluttered storage chamber. His heart was hammering so fast, he could hear it beating inside his head.

'... forty-nine, forty-eight, forty-seven ...'

Desperate to keep moving, Jake weaved his way through midnight blue barrels and crates to a hatch on the other side.

'... thirty, twenty-nine, twenty eight ...'

As he stepped into a different corridor, pilots and mechanics rushed past him. Jake lowered his head and pushed his way through the crowd.

'… eighteen, seventeen, sixteen …'

When he looked up, he saw a side entrance to the hangar deck. It was open and spilling thick black smoke. A damaged maintenance droid rolled out of the door, its shell dented and one of its arms hanging by a knot of wires.

'… ten, nine, eight …'

Jake raced forward.

'… seven, six, five …'

A warning light flashed above the door and it started to close.

'… four, three, two …'

Jake threw himself through the gap a second before the door snapped shut. He rolled on to the hangar deck floor and lay there, fighting for breath.

'… one,' said the voice. 'Inner doors sealed. Hangar deck purge commencing.'

Jake sat up. The burning wreckage of the *ISS Timidus* lay scattered around him. He could feel its heat on his face and hear the red hot debris cracking. No one was trying to put out the fire and Jake knew why. It was because the launch locks were about to open.

Not far away, he could see the plump hull of the *Dark Horse*. Kella, Nanoo and Kay were leaning out of the cargo hold.

'Hurry up,' cried Kella. 'We're closing the ramp.'

Amber lights started to flash above the launch lock doors. With a final burst of energy, Jake charged over to the cargo hauler and dived on to the rising ramp. The mighty lock doors opened in unison and Jake felt the temperature drop. He held on tight until the ramp closed.

'Where are the others?' he panted.

'They safe,' said Nanoo, helping Jake to his feet.

The *Dark Horse* shuddered as the oxygen was sucked from the hangar deck.

'Did you really fight Admiral Vantard?' asked Kay.

Jake nodded. 'We crossed swords. I was lucky to get away.'

'We had better get strapped in,' recommended Kella.

The four of them hurried to the guest quarters and strapped themselves to the narrow beds. Jake noticed that the mattresses were harder than ever and the pillows still stank like old socks.

The *Dark Horse* gathered speed as it passed through the launch lock doors and shot into space, like an overweight bullet. Through the porthole window, Jake could see naval shuttles and fighter craft tumbling alongside them. A scattering of empty crates and fuel cells richocheted off their hull.

'Why engine stop?' asked Nanoo.

Jake listened and his heart sank. Nanoo was right, the engine had stopped.

'Let's find out.'

The four of them unstrapped themselves and made their way to the top deck. It felt strange to be back aboard the *Dark Horse*, with only their magnetic gravity boots to hold them down. Manik had once told Jake that the cargo hauler had an artificial-gravity system installed, but Granny Leatherhead would not let the crew turn it on, because it used up too much energy.

As they entered the bridge, a stray gunship narrowly missed the window. Nichelle was sitting at the controls, while Farid leant over his scanner and Kodan squeezed into a secret compartment in the nose of the ship. Granny Leatherhead was slumped in the captain's chair, nursing her bruised face. Callidus and Capio stood nearest the door, holding on to wall straps. Jake knew that Scargus and Manik would be in the engine room, while Maaka and Woorak operated the sawn-off laser cannon on the gun deck.

It didn't matter how injured they were, the Space Dogs were born survivors. Jake had watched them fight their way out of other tight spots. If anyone could escape from the *ISS Magnificent*, it was this crew.

'Grubber me!' screeched a voice above them. 'Abandon ship! Abandon ship!'

It was Squawk, the parrot, perched on top of a metal cabinet and flapping his colourful wings.

'We found him in the engine room,' said Kay. 'I think he was pleased to see us.'

Granny Leatherhead noticed them standing in the doorway.

'What are you space pups doing on the bridge?' she demanded. 'We owe you big time for breaking us out, but we're not in the clear yet.'

'We want to know what's going on,' said Jake. 'Is there something wrong with the engine?'

'The engine's fine,' she croaked. 'We've turned it off, because we're hiding. If we're lucky, Admiral Vantard will be too busy putting out his fire to notice our ship drifting off with the other damaged craft. Now get to your posts. Kella in the medical bay, Nanoo in the engine room and Jake in the rear turret. We need to be ready in case we're spotted.'

'What about me?' asked Kay.

Granny Leatherhead eyed the pink-haired pirate with a crooked smile. 'Well, throttle my thrusters. I didn't see you there, Captain Jagger. Where's your ship?'

'It's safe, but my crew are swimming with the stars. I never did thank you for saving the *Divine Wind*.'

'If we get away from the *ISS Magnificent*, we can call it even.' Granny Leatherhead looked at Kay's new robotic eye. 'You're a brave girl, Kay. I reckon your dad would have been proud of you.'

Kay smirked. 'Don't go getting soft on me, you jolly codger.'

'Me? Never. I'll tell you what, you can stay on the bridge, if you promise not to get in my way. Who knows, you might learn a thing or two from an old Space Dog.' Granny Leatherhead turned to Jake, Kella and Nanoo. 'What are you three still doing here? Move your afts!'

It was as though they had never left. Jake raced along the top deck to the captain's quarters, while Kella and Nanoo disappeared down the metal staircase. Once he was through the black hatch door, Jake rolled over the captain's curved wooden bed and climbed up the narrow ladder between the two porthole windows, which led to a hidden turret overlooking the rear exhausts.

In the turret, Jake climbed on to the laser cannon saddle and gripped it with his knees. He powered up the weapon and opened the gun port. As the metal cover slid back, the laser cannon rolled forward and he was greeted by a strange sight. Nichelle had positioned the *Dark Horse* beneath a cluster of naval craft, many of which had been bashed and dented as they were sucked out of the launch locks. It was odd to see the naval shuttles and fighters in such a jumbled mess, when they were normally so neat and orderly. As he watched, the ships started to drift apart, breaking up the cover.

'Attention crew,' said Granny Leatherhead over the intercom. 'Scargus and Manik have patched up the boosters and we're going to make a run for it. I don't want any accidents, so hold on to something. We've been hurt enough already.'

Jake heard the engine fire up, and he clung on to the laser cannon. Granny Leatherhead's words repeated inside his head: *We've been hurt enough already.* The Space Dogs had clearly been tortured for information. Had he rescued them in time, or had they talked to save their own necks?

When Jake was on Altus, his top general, Rex Kent, had warned him that space pirates could not be trusted. 'Can they keep a secret?' Rex had asked. 'What if they were captured and tortured? Would they reveal our location?' Jake, Kella, Nanoo, Callidus, Capio and the Space Dogs were the only people outside the Tego Nebula to know the location of Altus. Not even Kay knew where to find it.

No, the crew would never betray him or the Altian people, would they? So why was Admiral Vantard heading to the seventh solar system? Was he joining his fleet for the attack, or had someone told him where to find Altus and its three crystal moons? With a sinking feeling, Jake held on to the laser cannon, while the cargo hauler tore across space to the trading station where the *Divine Wind* was waiting.

Whether Admiral Vantard knew about Altus or not, there were still other planets in the seventh solar system under attack. Jake and the fleet had to get there as quickly as possible. There wasn't a moment to lose.

Chapter 13

A Special Mission

'What's the matter?' asked Kella, when Jake eventually left his turret and trudged into the medical bay.

'Nothing,' he lied.

'Your face tells a different story,' she said, raising an eyebrow.

'I'm just sorry that I was unable to finish Admiral Vantard when I had the chance.'

Kella had been taking it in turns to heal herself and the crew, but now the medical bay was empty. Her skin looked much healthier and her breathing had returned to normal.

'Would it have changed anything if you had killed him?' she asked, removing the gold pendant from her face. 'The Interstellar Government would have found someone else, in the same way that Admiral Vantard replaced Admiral Nex.'

'It would have stopped him from reaching Altus,' he mumbled.

'Altus? What makes you think that he's heading there?'

Jake heard a noise in the corridor. He turned to find Scargus standing outside the door.

'Don't stop because of me,' said the chief engineer, peering at them through his thick glasses. 'I've come to see Kella about my leg.'

Jake stepped aside and forced a smile on to his face. 'It's OK, I can wait.'

Scargus scratched at his bushy grey beard, like a flea-bitten dog. 'You're worried that one of us squealed – eh, lad?'

Jake's smile faded and words spilled out of his mouth before he could stop them. 'Well, did you?'

If anything, he had expected Scargus to bark with laughter or shout with anger, but the chief engineer simply shrugged. 'I don't know.'

Scargus limped inside and sat on the edge of the bed, his body trembling and his eyes troubled.

'What happens in maximum interrogation?' asked Kella delicately.

Scargus shuddered. 'Pain, mostly, unlike anything you've ever experienced. And they call spacejackers animals! After a while, you barely know your own name, let alone what you're saying. If I didn't talk, then maybe one of the others did. But I doubt that any of us will remember.'

Kella glanced nervously at Jake and he could tell that she was thinking the same thing. If there had been one independent colony safe from the Interstellar Navy, it had been Altus. Now there was a good chance that Admiral Vantard knew its exact location.

'What's this all about?' demanded Granny Leatherhead, as she hobbled into the dining area on the first deck, clutching a flask of pirate tea. 'Who called a meeting on my ship?'

'I did,' said Jake, standing at the front with Kella, Nanoo and Kay.

The crew trickled into the room and took their seats, casting the four of them curious looks. Jake surveyed the familiar faces and he felt a rush of affection for his old shipmates. If one of them had betrayed Altus, he knew that they would not have done so easily. His eyes found Callidus and Capio, who smiled encouragingly at him.

'That's it, everyone's here,' said Farid. 'Nichelle has left the ship on autopilot, so this had better be quick.'

Jake nodded. 'OK, I'll cut to the chase. Once we collect the *Divine Wind*, I'll need to rejoin the

Independent Alliance. I'm going to lead the fleet to war and I could really do with your help.'

Granny Leatherhead frowned at him. 'And who says that we want to join your little armada, Kid Cutler? We're spacejackers, not warriors.'

'Jake just saved your life!' exclaimed Kay indignantly. 'You owe him.'

'Is that so?' said Granny Leatherhead. 'We've helped him out plenty of times. And he still owes each of us a crate of crystals. Besides, this is my ship and Jake knows my views on galactic war. Why should I care if the United Worlds and independent colonies want to kill each other?'

'How about your granddaughter?' asked Jake coolly.

Scargus had once told Jake how the captain's daughter, Jenny, had quit the crew to settle on Reus in the seventh solar system, where she married a respectable crystal dealer, before giving birth to her own daughter. Granny Leatherhead had been saving up for years, so she could retire from piracy and join her family, but during the battle with the *ISS Colossus*, the crew had been forced to throw the captain's gold overboard, so that the *Dark Horse* could escape the black hole.

Granny Leatherhead's single eye flashed with anger and she hurled her flask at the dining-area wall. 'What did you say?'

'You heard me,' said Jake, standing his ground. 'If we don't stop the Interstellar Navy, they'll wipe out the independent colonies, including Reus. I'll get you a crate of crystals, two if you want, but first you have to help me to end this war.'

Granny Leatherhead was now swaying unsteadily on the spot with her hand dangerously close to her laser pistol. 'What do you know about family, boy? You can't even remember your parents.'

'Hey, take it easy,' said Callidus, rising to his feet. 'We're all on the same side.'

'Don't you start,' she snapped. 'I'm the one who gives the orders aboard this cargo hauler.'

'Listen,' said Jake, firmly. 'We have to work together. If Admiral Vantard finds Altus, you can kiss your crystals goodbye forever.'

Granny Leatherhead drew her laser pistol and scratched her scalp with the barrel. 'What does the war have to do with Altus?'

Jake hesitated. How would the crew react to being accused of betrayal?

Scargus stood up and cleared his throat. 'We have reason to believe that Admiral Vantard has obtained information about the location of Altus,' said the chief engineer grumpily. 'And yes, I mean that one of us has probably blabbed.'

There was a ripple of protest, but no one seemed certain enough to deny it. Kodan appeared to be the most concerned, because, like Jake, he was a descendant of Captain Alyus Don, the space pirate king who discovered Altus, which meant that he was related to the Altian people.

'How do we stop the *ISS Magnificent*?' asked Callidus.

'We can't,' said Jake miserably. 'It's heading straight for the seventh solar system and the Independent Alliance is too slow to catch it.'

'The cyber-monks could send a message to Altus, if you tell them where to find it,' suggested Capio. 'That way, your people could evacuate the planet before the Interstellar Navy arrives.'

'Message not work,' said Nanoo. 'Signal not penetrate Tego Nebula.'

'He's right,' groaned Jake. 'Altus is completely surrounded by the nebula cloud. It's too thick and ionised with electricity for a message to get through.'

'Altus is inside the Tego Nebula?' piped up Kay. 'That's awesome!'

Jake looked around the room and realised that Kay was the only person who had never visited Altus.

Kella shook her head at how easily Jake and Nanoo had let slip its location. 'Is there nothing else we can do?'

Jake shrugged. It seemed hopeless.

Granny Leatherhead lowered her pistol. 'I'm sorry, Jake. That's too bad.'

Jake raised his eyebrows. 'I didn't think you cared.'

The captain chewed her next words carefully, before spitting them out. 'We'll accompany you back to your fleet, but that's as far as we go. The *Dark Horse* is not a warship and the crew is in no condition to fight. You'll have to manage without us.'

With that, Granny Leatherhead shuffled from the dining area and disappeared up the metal staircase, assisted by Kodan. Jake remained standing as the rest of the crew returned to their posts. Callidus and Capio stayed behind.

'What are we going to do?' asked Jake. 'The Altian people have no idea that they're in danger.'

'We may not be able to save your planet,' said Callidus, 'but by Zerost we'll make the Interstellar Navy pay for every life it takes from Altus, or any other independent colony.'

The two men left the room and Jake strapped himself into the nearest seat. There had to be a way to warn Rex Kent and the Altian planetary guard. All he had to do was think of it.

'Pirate tea?' asked Kella, heading to the kitchen area.

Jake nodded glumly.

'It OK, we think of something,' said Nanoo cheerily.

But after several hours and numerous flasks of tea, they had still not come up with a way of contacting Altus.

When the *Dark Horse* eventually reached the trading station on the edge of the fifth solar system, Jake walked over to the nearest porthole window and spotted the *Divine Wind* waiting patiently for them. As much as he enjoyed being back on the cargo hauler, he would keep his promise to Kay and return to the yellow star frigate with Kella, Nanoo, Callidus and Capio. At least the Space Dogs would stay with them until they rejoined the fleet.

'Come on,' he said to the others. 'We had better get ready to go.'

Nichelle steered the ship into an empty docking bay and the crew gathered in the cargo hold. It was sad to leave the *Dark Horse* so soon, perhaps for the last time.

'So you're serious about this, eh?' asked Granny Leatherhead, as she lowered the loading ramp. 'You're going to take on the entire Interstellar Navy to save a load of clueless colonists?'

'Yes,' said Jake, determinedly. 'I signed a treaty to unite the independent colonies and that's what I'm going to do.'

The captain stared at him, but this time her grey eye sparkled. 'You're a good lad, Jake.'

'Thanks.' Jake was shocked to see a tear roll steadily down Granny Leatherhead's cheek, leaving a glistening trail across her rumpled skin.

'I want to thank you for saving me and the crew,' she croaked humbly. 'There aren't many people who would have rescued us from a naval warship. A few more days and we would have been kalmar bait. Kay's right, we owe you one, and I wish that there was something we could do to help, other than fight.'

'You would have done the same for me,' he said modestly.

'I doubt it,' she cackled, turning to Callidus and Capio. 'And I'm sorry for kicking you two off the ship a few weeks back. I know that you were only trying to protect Jake, but there was no way I was going to surrender to Admiral Vantard.'

'That's OK,' said Callidus. 'We know that a Space Dog's bark is worse than its bite. Take care of yourself, captain. Keep an eye on the stars and stay out of trouble.'

'Don't worry about us, there's no way that we're going to get ourselves captured again. At the first whiff of danger, we'll use Nanoo's boosters to escape. I reckon we're one of the fastest ships in the galaxy now.'

'That's it!' cried Jake. 'That's how you can help.'

Granny Leatherhead stared at him, as though he had spoken in Gorkish. 'How will running away help?'

Jake felt a rush of excitement as a plan formed inside his head. 'No, not run away. I want you to go on a special mission. The *Dark Horse* is fast enough to beat the *ISS Magnificent* to the seventh solar system.'

Farid looked nervous. 'What use will that be? We won't be able to stop the naval fleet on our own.'

'I know, but at least you can warn the Altian people.'

'You want us to return to Altus?' exclaimed Granny Leatherhead. 'Now wait a minute, the last time we were there, those backward bumpkins tried to seize our ship.'

'Rex will listen to you,' said Jake. 'I know it's asking a lot, but thousands of lives could be in danger. Altus is the only independent colony that doesn't know about the galactic war. We have to give my people a fighting chance.'

Kodan stepped forward and nodded his approval.

Granny Leatherhead groaned. 'The Space Dogs haven't lasted this long by helping other folk. We don't owe that planet a thing.'

'You may not be from Altus,' said Callidus, 'but your ancestors were from Zerost, the same as the Altian people. Are you really going to let the Interstellar Navy finish the job it started hundreds of years ago, by allowing Admiral Vantard to murder your fellow space pirates and their families?'

Granny Leatherhead glanced around the cargo hold at her crew. A few of them shrugged, but most of them joined Kodan in showing their support. Jake figured that they were voting with their conscience, especially those who feared they had given away the planet's location.

The captain cursed. 'OK, fine, we'll accept your special mission and deliver your message. But if that poxy Protectorate orders our arrest, I'm going to shoot them myself.'

'Fair enough,' said Jake, spitting on his hand and holding it out. 'Thank you, captain.'

Granny Leatherhead shook hands to seal the deal.

'Well, rattle my rivets,' she croaked. 'I never thought that I would be the one in my family doing something noble. Now get off my ship, before you have any more bright ideas that I might regret.'

Chapter 14

The Scout Ship

Back inside the trading station, Jake thanked the traders for looking after the *Divine Wind* and for watching over the prisoners. Captain Wortus and his naval troopers were being held in a secure storage room in the depths of the station.

'I want you to keep them here,' said Jake. 'While we're gone.'

'For how long?' protested the chief trader, who was a tall woman with short black hair. 'Food and water is too precious to waste on kalmar farts like them.'

'Not long,' promised Jake. 'When I return from the seventh solar system, we can find them a proper prison.'

'People are angry with the Interstellar Navy,' she said, clutching her new plasma rifle. 'Some of the traders have family on Vantos. We should make this lot walk the airlock.'

Jake looked at the hardened faces around him. 'I know these troopers treated you badly, but you're better than them. We have to stay strong. Let the Independent Alliance fight this war.'

The chief trader reluctantly agreed, and she escorted Jake back to the *Divine Wind*. He boarded the ship and found the others waiting on the bridge.

'Ahoy there, shipmates,' he said. 'Are we ready to hit the stars?'

'Aye,' cheered Kay heartily.

Jake took his seat at the controls and checked the display.

'Good news,' said Callidus. 'We have the Independent Alliance on the long-range scanner. I've sent a message to Father Benedict to let him know that our mission was a success.'

Jake smiled. 'In that case, let's get ready to blast off.'

Kella, Nanoo, Callidus and Capio hurried to their posts and strapped themselves in, while Kay settled herself in the captain's chair.

'Ready when you are, Kid Cutler,' she said.

Jake released the thrusters and the *Divine Wind* pulled smoothly away from the trading station, before soaring into open space alongside the *Dark Horse*. It felt good to be back in control and Jake rolled the old star frigate in celebration. He knew what was waiting for them in the seventh solar system, but he wasn't afraid. If nothing else, he would show the galaxy that the Independent Alliance was prepared to stand up to the Interstellar Government.

The two pirate ships met the fleet as it entered the fifth solar system. Jake hailed the other captains and explained that they had rescued the *Dark Horse* from the Interstellar Navy.

'We were able to damage the *ISS Magnificent* at the same time,' he added, before releasing the communicator.

'You risked the mission for a crew of space pirates?' exclaimed Captain Swan, his surprise ringing through the speakers.

'What use is a battered old cargo hauler?' asked Captain Harley.

'It looks like a stray asteroid,' sniffed Captain Quinn. 'I suppose we could always use it for target practice.'

'That ship has seen more action than this entire fleet,' said Jake, pressing his mouth to the communicator. 'It destroyed the *ISS Colossus* and the *Black Death*, not to mention a squadron of Gork fighter craft.'

There was a stunned silence and Jake imagined the captains taking a closer look at their display screens.

'That'll teach them to judge a craft by its hull,' whispered Kay.

'But the *Dark Horse* won't be travelling with us,' informed Jake, 'because I'm sending it on a special mission to save thousands of lives. So the next time you see its crew, I suggest that you show them a bit more respect.'

'Aye, my lord,' said the captains.

Jake had been quick to defend the Space Dogs. As he watched the *Dark Horse* disappear into the distance, he couldn't help but wonder if Granny Leatherhead would keep her word and return to Altus. Was he expecting too much? He trusted that crew with his life, and he hoped that they would do the right thing. It just wasn't in their nature to be heroes.

Callidus entered the bridge. 'How's it going up here?'

'Great,' said Jake. 'We've got plenty of fuel cells and two days to get to Libertina in the sixth solar system.'

'Excellent, but let's keep an eye …'

'… on the stars, and stay out of trouble?' finished Jake.

Callidus seemed taken aback. 'Actually, I was going to say: keep an eye on the scanners for enemy craft and space storms.'

'Oh,' said Jake. 'It's just that you say the other thing a lot. That reminds me, I found the exact same phrase on a plaque in Papa Don's spaceport. It was like his family motto or something.'

'Really?' Callidus sounded intrigued.

'Have you ever worked for the space mafia?' wondered Jake.

'Not as far as I know. It's just a saying, that's all.'

'That's not all,' said Jake. 'Papa Don's family crest is the symbol of Altus. His family descended from Calpus Don, the son of Captain Alyus Don.'

'You mean the pirate king, Alyus Don?'

'Yes,' said Jake, recalling what Papa Don had told him. 'Calpus Don left Altus in protest after his father died, because his sister Katrina took over as ruler. Katrina had already married her father's first mate, Jago Cutler, which is why all of the rulers since have had that name.'

Callidus tilted his head curiously. 'What are you trying to say?'

'Don't you see?' Jake was quickly piecing together the facts in his mind. 'Papa Don's family motto could have been passed down from Captain Alyus Don, the same as his family crest, which might mean that you first heard it on Altus.'

'You think it's further proof that I'm Andras Cutler?' said Callidus. 'Perhaps an old memory lurking in my subconscious?'

Jake shrugged. 'Why not?'

Callidus smiled kindly. 'It's a nice theory, but I probably picked it up in Papa Don's or heard it from another fortune seeker.'

Jake was forced to accept that the words didn't prove anything on their own. Would they ever find out for certain if Callidus was his father? How much evidence did Jake need? He had already missed so much already; was he prepared to wait another eleven years to be sure? The more he thought about it, the more the idea grew on him, and he found it hard to think about Andras Cutler without picturing Callidus. If Jake was honest, he secretly hoped that the fortune seeker was his father. Callidus was a good man and someone he cared deeply about. But hoping wasn't enough. Jake had to know the truth.

For the next two days, the Independent Alliance moved steadily closer to the sixth solar system, keeping watch for enemy craft and steering clear of space storms. Several other vessels had joined them on the way, including two cargo haulers from Gazear and a travelling circus ship. They had even picked up a Gork fortune seeker called Tark, who worshipped Mother Universe, the creator of everything. Jake had offered to pay Tark for his services, but the Gork had refused, claiming that he wanted to fight for independence. Captain Swan had asked him if he was prepared to kill his own species, to which Tark had bared his needle-thin teeth and replied: 'Are *you*?'

While the new crews were encouraging, Jake knew that their success would depend on how many independent warships were waiting at Libertina. Without the stellar-net, there was no way of knowing how many colonies had responded to his call for help.

Jake was spending so much time at the helm, he was fast becoming a skilled pilot. He had only let Callidus take over the controls when he had needed a break. Apart from that, it had been mostly just Kay and Jake on the bridge. Nanoo had used the time to tinker with the engine and the shields, while Kella finished healing herself in the medical bay. It would have taken a normal person weeks to recover, but now, only days since her accident, it was hard to tell that she had ever been burnt.

Kella joined them briefly on the bridge as they passed by her home planet, Haven, in the sixth solar system. In silence, she stared out of the window, before returning to the medical bay. Jake caught her pained reflection in the glass and knew that she was missing her family.

Callidus and Capio spent most of their time camped out on the gun deck, ready to fire the laser cannon. To Jake's surprise, Capio had borrowed his handheld computer to learn about the cyber-monks. Apparently, Capio was fascinated by the idea that people would dedicate their lives to technology, and he wanted to read some old research files written by Father Pius. Jake could understand why a life of peace would appeal to someone who had once fought a space monster.

Radio Interference kept the fleet updated with the latest developments, including reports of attacks on civilian ships by Gork patrols. In one broadcast, Father Benedict shared a rumour that a small independent colony in the second solar system had been bombed. He also informed them that naval warships had surrounded the Tego Nebula in the seventh, which the cyber-abbot assumed had something to do with Papa Don's illegal spaceport. This news made Jake wonder if the *Dark Horse* had made it to Altus in time. He checked his display and activated the communicator.

'Attention, all ships, this is Jake Cutler. We're approaching Libertina, so I want you to stay alert. It's a miracle that we've made it this far without being spotted.'

'Aye, my lord.'

But Jake had spoken too soon. Within minutes, he was contacted by Tark from his converted racing ship, the *Half Moon*.

'Ahoy, *Divine Wind*,' said the deep, strangled voice. 'I thought that you should know we're being watched.'

Kay checked the long-range scanner. 'I can't see any other ships.'

'Ahoy, *Half Moon*,' said Jake. 'Are you sure? We're not picking up anything.'

Tark rasped with laughter. 'It's a Gork scout ship, which is small and difficult to detect. If you look in the direction of the third solar system, you will see it positioned between the planets Astrasia and Quar. We need to stop that ship before it can report back to the naval fleet.'

Jake fiddled with his display screen until he found the scout ship. It was a tiny, midnight blue sphere with a single exhaust, not much bigger than an escape pod. As he watched, the scout ship turned and fled.

'It's making a run for it,' he said, flicking a switch on the communicator. 'Attention, fleet. Hold your course. We've spotted a Gork scout ship and I'm going after it.'

Chapter 15

Libertina

Jake accelerated after the scout ship, which was surprisingly fast, but the *Divine Wind* was faster. The star frigate soon caught up with the tiny sphere, as it made for a nearby asteroid field.

Jake activated the intercom. 'Cal, Capio, we need to take out that Gork scout.'

'Understood,' said Callidus.

The sound of laser cannon fire filled the speakers and a stream of laser bolts burst from the gun deck. Most of the shots hit surrounding asteroids, which exploded into clouds of dust. Kay squealed with delight at the power of her new weapons.

'Nanoo, you're spoiling me,' she chirped merrily.

'We're running out of time, Cal,' warned Jake, as they drew closer to the asteroid field.

'It's no good,' said the fortune seeker. 'That ship is too small to catch in our gunsights.'

'OK, then we'll have to ram it.'

Jake ignored the increasing number of rocks around them and focused on the scout ship. As he closed in, he could make out the fin-headed Gork pilot curled up inside it.

CRASH!

'Watch it,' yelled Kay, as a small asteroid bounced off the hull.

The scout ship changed course, veering sharply away from the asteroid field.

'Blast! I almost had it,' said Jake, turning the *Divine Wind* to follow.

CRASH!

The *Divine Wind* hit another asteroid.

'Jake …'

'I know, I know. I'm sorry.'

'It's not that,' said Kay. 'We're near the meeting point at Libertina.'

Jake's heart skipped a beat. It was the moment that he had been waiting for; the moment when he would find out if his message had worked; the moment of truth.

'Are there any ships waiting?' he asked eagerly.

'Aye, three warships.'

'Three?' Jake groaned with disappointment. 'Is that all?'

Kay nodded. 'And the scout ship is heading straight for them.'

Jake watched the small sphere curve around the large green planet to where the warships were waiting on the other side. 'At least it's trapped.'

But as the *Divine Wind* chased the scout ship around Libertina, Kay frowned suspiciously at the scanner.

'I don't like this,' she said. 'We should wait for the rest of the fleet.'

'There's no time …'

It was too late. Jake spotted three large vessels orbiting the planet, but they had not been sent by the independent colonies.

Kay looked up and hissed like an angry cat. 'Gork warships.'

Jake stared in alarm at the bloated midnight blue hulls and open gun ports of the three Gork warships as they skimmed the atmosphere of Libertina. 'That's not good.'

'Where are the independent colony ships?' asked Kay in disbelief. 'I can't believe that no one turned up.'

'Never mind that now,' said Jake, tugging the controls. 'We've got to get out of here.'

There was no way that the star frigate could take on three warships single-handed. The *Divine Wind* twisted away from the planet as the Gorks opened fire. A shot caught its underside, but the laser failed to penetrate the reinforced shields.

'That Nanoo is a genius,' marvelled Kay.

Jake squeezed the thrusters, and the *Divine Wind* accelerated away from Libertina, while Callidus and Capio returned fire. 'We have to get back to the fleet.'

'Agreed, but you're going the wrong way,' said Kay, poking the scanner with her finger.

'What?' Jake checked his instruments and saw that she was right. 'We'll have to find a way to circle back around those warships.'

'Make it quick,' she said. 'I've picked up more craft dead ahead.'

'How many?'

'I don't know exactly … Loads.' Kay smacked the side of her robotic eye, as though trying to get it to focus. 'It could be twenty or thirty ships?'

Jake twisted in his seat. 'Are you sure? That sounds like half the naval fleet.'

What did this mean? Had the Interstellar Navy conquered the seventh solar system already and they were now attacking the sixth?

'I thought you wanted to fight them,' said Kay. 'Does it matter which solar system we die in?'

'We're not going to die.' Jake gritted his teeth. 'Not unless we can take those wretchards with us.'

Kay laughed nervously. 'And you were worried about a scout ship.'

A laser bolt streamed past the window from the pursuing Gork warships.

'How long before we're out of firing range?' asked Jake, rolling the *Divine Wind*.

'We'll run into the other vessels first,' said Kay.

Jake squinted at the display screen. He could make out a mass of muddled shapes in the distance, like a multicoloured mountain of metal.

Muddled?

Multicoloured?

'Magnifty!' he cheered.

Kay looked bemused. 'Jake?'

The *Divine Wind* was heading straight for the heart of the incoming fleet. But instead of an orderly formation of vessels that indicated the Interstellar Navy, it was an unruly cluster of mismatched spacecraft. Jake feasted his eyes on the colourful hulls and unique markings. He could make out at least thirty warships, gunships and other large craft, escorted by swarms of fighters.

'It's the rest of our fleet,' he said, bursting with excitement.

'Well, scrap my scanner!' whooped Kay. 'They came, they actually came.'

Jake activated the communicator. 'Ahoy there, independent colony ships, this is Jake Cutler aboard the *Divine Wind* star frigate. We need help urgently.'

The speakers crackled for a moment and then several voices spoke out at once in a confused chorus.

'Ahoy there, *Divine Wind* …'

'Ahoy, Jake Cutler …'

'Ahoy, my lord …'

'… this is General Juan Da Silva of the Libertina planetary guard …'

'… Commander Owen Heart from Earrant …'

'… Captain Chui Jia from Ho Dan …'

'… at your service.'

'… awaiting your orders.'

'… ready to fight.'

'Ahoy there, kiddo, how can we help?'

Jake recognised the last voice. It was his friend, Baden Scott, aboard his salvage trawler, the *Rough Diamond III*. Baden and his crew had assisted Jake and the Space Dogs following the battle of the black hole.

'We're being chased by three Gork warships,' said Jake.

'How rude,' joked the salvage captain. 'Don't they know that this is a private party?'

'We shall attack immediately,' said a gruff voice.

Several vessels broke away from the fleet and opened fire on the enemy. Jake watched the Gork warships almost collide in their attempt to flee, while chubby fighter craft trickled from their launch locks. The wide warship hulls were tough to penetrate, but there was no escaping the flood of laser bolts. Jake turned the *Divine Wind* around and joined in the attack, soaring beneath the nearest Gork vessel, while Callidus and Capio ripped a hole in its belly. A white space clipper fired something into the opening and within seconds the warship exploded.

Kay looked perplexed. 'That clipper is a pirate ship. How did they get your message?'

'Word must be getting around,' said Jake, pulling hard on the controls to avoid hitting a Gork fighter. 'Father Benedict is probably contacting every friendly ship in the area.'

'Friendly?' snorted Kay. 'That's not how I would describe them. Mind you, at least they're not from the United Worlds.'

Jake glanced at the screen and caught sight of an old space tug surrounded by Gork fighters. Its hull proudly displayed a robot skull over two crossed spanners.

'It's *Rusty's Revenge*!' said Jake, changing direction. 'The Hacker Jackers are in trouble.'

The Hacker Jackers were a pirate crew of free robots led by an eight-foot battle droid named Vigor-8. Jake had helped the robot captain to escape from Papa Don's, which had earned him its gratitude. In return, Vigor-8 had saved Jake's life and delivered him safely to the gathering on Santanova.

'What are you going to do?' asked Kay.

With no time to form a strategy, Jake flew the *Divine Wind* into the midst of the chubby Gork fighters, forcing them to scatter out of the way. Callidus and Capio blasted several of them at short range, and they burst like bubbles. This freed up *Rusty's Revenge* to take out two more, before the rest of the fighters retreated.

Jake activated the communicator. 'Ahoy, *Rusty's Revenge*. Are you OK?'

'Ahoy, *Divine Wind*,' responded the deep electronic voice of Vigor-8. 'Greetings, Jake Cutler. My crew is fully operational, thank you. We have lost life support, but that is not a problem for robots. I watched your speech at the gathering and we received your message. The Hacker Jackers will help you to fight the Interstellar Navy, unless this is a matter only for humans.'

'Thanks, Vigor-8,' said Jake. 'I would be honoured to fight alongside you.'

At that very moment a second Gork warship exploded, showering the fleet with debris. Jake saw a faded pink gunship collide with a large section of hull, while at the same time a long purple fighter lost power. This distraction allowed the third Gork warship to make its escape. Jake was quick to pursue, closely followed by a bulky green warship called the *Sol Dorado*, which bore the flag of Libertina.

Without the stellar-net, the only way for the Gorks to warn the naval fleet would be for them to join the naval warships in the seventh solar system, where they could use their short-range communicators. But Jake wasn't going to let the Gorks ruin the surprise, if he could help it.

The Gork warship fired its rear laser cannon, forcing Jake and the *Sol Dorado* to veer sharply. It wasn't until they had reached Libertina that they were able to get a clear shot. Callidus and Capio targeted the Gork warship's exhausts, while the *Sol Dorado* attempted to take out its weapons, but the Gork pilot was slippier than starweed.

'We need to hurry,' warned Kay. 'I'm picking up more ships on the long-range scanner.'

'It's OK,' said Jake. 'I've been expecting them and it's not the Interstellar Navy.'

The *Star Chaser* appeared on their display screen, leading the rest of the Independent Alliance, which now boasted ten armour-plated passenger ships, two Shan-Ti warships, two cargo haulers, a travelling circus ship, a converted racing ship and a handful of Santanova fighter craft.

'Ahoy, *Divine Wind*,' greeted Captain Swan over the communicator. 'I see that you've engaged the enemy already. Do you need any assistance?'

'Ahoy, *Star Chaser*,' said Jake. 'Yes, stop that warship!'

The Gork vessel was trapped. Jake eased off the thrusters and the *Divine Wind* dropped back. He wanted the other crews to have some battle experience before they reached the seventh solar system. As he watched, the passenger ships attempted to encircle the Gork warship, but there were too many of them, and they had to swerve to avoid hitting each other. Those that managed to squeeze into position exchanged laser cannon fire with the Gorks for several long minutes, before the warship finally succumbed to greater numbers.

'We did it!' Kay climbed on to the scanner and performed a hip-shaking victory dance. 'I can't believe we destroyed three Gork warships.'

Jake laughed nervously. He knew that they had been lucky not to lose more of their own craft. At best, his fleet was clumsy and disorganised, but he had a different word for it.

'That was a shambles,' he said. 'We had no strategy, no structure and no teamwork. I'm surprised we didn't shoot each other. If that's what we're like against three Gork warships, we're going to need some serious practice before we take on a whole naval fleet. Do we even know if the scout ship was inside one of those warships, or did it get away?'

Kay shrugged.

Kella hurried on to the bridge, clutching Jake's gold pendant. 'Are you two hurt? Do you need me to heal anything?'

'We're fine,' said Kay. 'Apart from Jake thinking the fleet is a mess.'

'He's right.' Callidus entered the room, followed by Capio and Nanoo. 'But what did you expect? I thought we did OK for a brand new fleet. On the positive side, we must have almost fifty ships now, plus a hundred fighters, which is more than we dared to hope. Unfortunately, we're still outnumbered and we need to get our act together fast, otherwise Admiral Vantard will wipe the stars with us.'

'What we do?' asked Nanoo.

'I'll call an emergency meeting with the other captains,' said Jake. 'We can use the ballroom aboard the *Star Chaser*. It's time to get organised.'

Chapter 16

The Seventh Solar System

Jake and Kay were the last to board the *Star Chaser*. Callidus had offered to go with them, but Jake had asked him to remain behind on the *Divine Wind* in case more Gork warships showed up. However, when Captain Swan escorted Jake and Kay into the ballroom, Jake wished that he had brought the ex-naval officer. The people waiting there were soldiers, not politicians. Jake could tell instantly by their surly expressions that the meeting was going to be very different to the gathering on Santanova.

The ballroom was wide and circular with a high glass ceiling, which provided a spectacular view of the stars. Its curved walls were meticulously decorated and lit by crystal chandeliers. A few tables were scattered around the edge of the room, where most of the captains waited with their first mates.

Jake stood before the group of hardy men and women, who stared intently back at him. Their spacesuits varied in colour and design, as though they had stepped out of a spacewear catalogue. A few of them had impressive scars or artificial body parts. The Gork fortune seeker was particularly alarming with his vacant black eyes, rubbery blue skin, and mangled headfin. But Jake was heartened to see a few familiar faces in the crowd, such as Baden Scott and Vigor-8.

'Thank you for coming,' he said. 'It's incredible that so many of you have answered my call to arms. I know it must have been hard for you to leave your planets and families –'

'Is this going to be another speech?' interrupted a large man with a gruff voice, who had a powerful robot jaw and a shiny grey Afro that resembled steel wool. A row of gold stars and a bronze name plate decorated his vibrant green uniform. It was General Juan Da Silva from the Libertina planetary guard. 'The time for talk is over. I came here to fight.'

'In that case, I'll get straight to the point,' said Jake, clearing his throat. 'We're about to take on the entire Interstellar Navy, something that has never been done before, and not all of us will survive. But this is our best chance to stop the Interstellar Government from taking over our colonies, and giving the Galactic Trade Corporation unlimited access to our crystal mines.'

'Are you really the ruler of Altus?' asked a square-faced man with curly blond hair, who had *Captain Heart* written on his chest under the flag of Earrant.

'Yes, but –'

'Do you have a crown?' asked a fierce-looking woman with jet black hair and a swamp brown uniform, who Jake assumed was Captain Chui Jia from Ho Dan.

'No, but –'

'So where is this Altus?' asked Tark, the Gork.

'Let the boy speak,' said Baden, who was wearing his dirty orange exploration suit and standing beside two other salvage captains. 'My home planet is Vantos and I'd like to know how we're going to save it.'

'Why should we take orders from a teenage spacejacker?' argued General Da Silva. 'I'm grateful that he's united the colonies, but does that make him the best person to lead us to war? How much battle experience does he have?'

'Hey, tin-chin, stop clanking your motor mouth and listen up,' said Kay heatedly. 'Jake Cutler has fought more warships than the lot of you put together. Who do you think stopped Admiral Nex and Scarabus Shark? If you've got a problem with him leading the Independent Alliance, you know where to find the airlock.'

General Da Silva glared furiously at Kay. His icy blue eyes raked her colourful pirate clothes, like a predator sizing up its prey. It was well known that the Libertina planetary guard was one of the toughest in the galaxy.

'This isn't about me,' said Jake quickly. 'This is about saving the independent colonies. You're right, General Da Silva. I still have a lot to learn, which is why I need your help. This fleet lacks organisation and leadership. Will you be my second-in-command?'

'Jake?' hissed Kay. 'What are you doing?'

'Second-in-command?' repeated General Da Silva, rubbing his robot jaw.

'Yes,' said Jake. 'We'll organise the fleet together. If anything happens to me, I want you to lead the Independent Alliance and finish the job. What do you say?'

A few of the captains nodded their approval, including Captain Heart and Captain Jia. But Kay scowled and folded her arms.

General Da Silva barked with laughter. 'Aye, my lord. Just keep that pink-haired pirate out of my way.'

'Thank you, general,' said Jake. 'Our first job is to come up with a plan of attack, but we don't have long. I want to leave for the seventh solar system within the hour, because we've got independent colonies to rescue.'

The plan they formed was far from perfect, but at least everyone knew what to do. General Da Silva and the captains had identified their different strengths and how they could work together. Jake was confident that this would make them a more effective fighting force. His head hurt from the intense discussions, where each of the captains had wanted to do things their own way. Callidus would probably have described this as a test of Jake's leadership skills, though there had been moments when he'd felt more like a referee.

Jake walked back to the airlock with Baden Scott.

'How come you're here?' he asked.

'It's nice to see you too,' laughed the salvage captain. 'What can I say? I heard about your message and I wanted to help my home planet. There comes a time when even I have to make a stand. It's not all bad, at least there will be plenty of work for my crew when the war is over.'

'I thought you were stuck in a service port. How did you pay off your docking fees?'

'I had to leave the dock master the key to my holiday home on Reus. He wasn't entirely happy, but it was the best that I could do under the circumstances. What about you? I couldn't believe it when you appeared on the *Interstellar News* at the gathering. Do I want to know how you got the golden cutlass away from Papa Don?'

'No,' said Jake, rubbing the scars on his chest where Papa Don's robot parrot had sunk its razor-sharp talons.

Baden popped a wad of chewing gum into his mouth. 'I thought not.'

The two of them reached the airlock.

Jake turned to the scruffy salvage captain. 'Thanks, Baden.'

'For what?'

'Doing the right thing.'

Baden smiled and Jake returned to the *Divine Wind*. Once back aboard the star frigate, he entered the bridge and took his seat at the controls.

'How did it go?' asked Callidus.

'General Da Silva is going to be my second-in-command,' said Jake. 'We've come up with a plan of attack and I really think we have a chance of beating the Interstellar Navy. The captains have loads of useful experience and their warships are packing some serious laserpower.'

Callidus nodded approvingly. 'And don't forget, there are other planetary guards already resisting the naval fleet in the seventh solar system. It might just be enough to give us the advantage.'

'There's only one way to find out,' said Jake, gripping the controls. 'Let's go and save the galaxy.'

The *Divine Wind* led the fleet away from Libertina and into open space. It would take them the best part of a day to reach the seventh solar system. As much as Jake worried that Admiral Vantard was heading for Altus, the captains had agreed that Vantos should be their first destination, as it had been holding out the longest against the Interstellar Navy.

The communicator crackled to life.

'Ahoy there, Independent Alliance,' said Father Benedict. 'This is Radio Interference with some urgent news. There has been movement in the seventh solar system. The naval warships have withdrawn from the independent colonies. It's not clear why they have broken off their attack. However, we do know that the ceasefire was ordered by Admiral Vantard himself. There is now a large concentration of warships by the Tego Nebula, which makes no strategic sense.'

Jake glanced at Callidus and Kay. 'Altus?'

'That's not all,' said the cyber-abbot. 'The Interstellar Navy knows that you're coming, Jake. We've picked up communications from a Gork scout ship, which has reported sightings of independent colony vessels in the sixth solar system.'

'Blast!' shouted Jake, accidentally knocking an empty tea flask on to the floor.

'There goes our element of surprise,' groaned Kay, shooting the air with her finger.

'And finally,' said Father Benedict. 'Papa Don has refused to surrender to the Interstellar Navy. However, he has agreed that the space mafia will remain neutral and not interfere with the war. From what we can gather, the naval fleet will leave him alone until they have finished with the independent colonies. That's it for now. We'll be in touch with any further developments.'

Jake was disappointed to hear that the space mafia was not taking sides, because they would have made a powerful ally. What was Papa Don playing at?

'Doesn't that miserable mobster realise the naval warships will come back for him?' grumbled Jake.

'I expect that he's buying himself some time, before he has to abandon his illegal spaceport,' said Callidus. 'He does have his guests to consider.'

'Guests?' scoffed Kay. 'More like cowardly criminals. I bet that Captain Hawker and his Starbucklers are hiding inside there, waiting until it's safe to come out. Not so tough now, eh?'

'I'm glad that the Interstellar Navy has ceased attacking the independent colonies,' said Callidus. 'But it was unwise of Admiral Vantard to move his fleet to the Tego Nebula, because the warship computers and shields will be affected by the static, putting them at a disadvantage. I've never known a nebula cloud so ionised with electricity.'

'Admiral Vantard has to be going after Altus,' said Jake. 'Why else would he risk everything? One of the Space Dogs must have given away its location. We need to hurry, before he takes Altus and then resumes his attack on the other colonies.'

Jake activated the communicator and hailed the other captains. After a brief discussion, they agreed that the Independent Alliance should change course to the Tego Nebula and confront the naval fleet.

'There's no point delaying what we've come here to do,' said General Da Silva gruffly. 'It's time to stop sneaking around this galaxy and fight these wretchards head-on.'

And with that, the fleet set course for the Tego Nebula.

The whole crew joined Jake and Kay on the bridge as the *Divine Wind* entered the seventh solar system. It was a significant moment and one they wanted to witness together. Jake could sense the tension in the room. Their fleet was only a few hours away from the enemy and the biggest space battle in history.

Kay kept an eye on the long-range scanner, but the naval warships remained stationed by the Tego Nebula. Jake had no idea if the *Dark Horse* had made it to Altus, or if the Altian people had escaped. Were they all trapped inside the Tego Nebula together?

Callidus appeared lost in thought and Jake wondered what must be going through his mind. If the fortune seeker really was his father and the true ruler of Altus, it would be his people in danger as well. Jake remembered what it was like not knowing who he was or where he was from. If only he could find a way to prove that Callidus was Andras Cutler, for both of their sakes. Jake would be more than happy to hand over the burden of leadership and let someone else rule Altus for a while.

In the distance, the planets basked in the warm sunlight. It was strange to be back in his home solar system. Everything looked the same to Jake, but somehow it felt different, as though it had been contaminated by a vile poison. His eye caught sight of a service port drifting through the stars. As they drew nearer, he recognised it as the place where they had first met Baden Scott, only now it was a lifeless wreck.

'Grubber me!' exclaimed Kay, when the extent of the damage became clear.

Jake stared in shock at the countless holes that riddled the blackened port. It looked as though it had been savaged long after the lights went out. How many people had been inside those metal walls when the hull breached and the fuel cells exploded?

'Gorks,' deduced Callidus, with a look of revulsion.

Nanoo held on to his neck slits, as though he might be sick. 'The Novu never hurt innocent people.'

Kella turned her face away from the window. 'If this is what they do to a defenceless service port, what will they do to the independent colonies?'

Jake now realised what they were facing. It was the ugly truth of war, and the reason they had to stop the Interstellar Government. Until now, it had seemed like an adventure, a mighty crusade for good, but looking at the mangled remains of the service port, it made him wonder what other horrors awaited them, especially with Altus only a few hours away.

The crew stood in silence, out of respect for the dead.

'Ships ahoy,' interrupted Kay, checking her scanner. 'And they're heading straight for us.'

Chapter 17

The Battle of the Tego Nebula

Jake tore his eyes from the wrecked service port. 'How many?'

'Three craft,' said Kay. 'But they're way too small to be warships.'

Jake alerted General Da Silva and the other captains. 'Attention, all ships. We've got incoming craft. Hold fire until we can identify them, but if they turn out to be Gork gunships, feel free to rip the rivets off them.'

'Aye, my lord,' said General Da Silva.

'With pleasure,' added Baden.

The three craft appeared on the display screen and Jake was relieved to see that they were not Gork gunships, but planetary guard vessels. With a burst of excitement, he recognised their black-and-white-chequered markings. The ships had come from Remota, the planet where he had grown up.

'Ahoy there, independent colony fleet,' hailed a familiar voice over the communicator. 'Do you have room for three more ships?'

Jake could hardly believe his ears. It was not a voice that he had been expecting.

'Ahoy there, Orana,' he said, grinning. 'Welcome to the Independent Alliance. I don't suppose you brought any apples with you?'

The last time that Jake had seen Orana, she had been a security guard in the space docks on Remota, which was located below the cyber-monk monastery at the bottom of Temple Hill.

'Is that you, Jakester?'

'Aye,' he said. 'I finally got my wish to see a naval warship. When did you join the planetary guard?'

'It was probably around the same time that you became a space pirate and the ruler of Altus. What happened to the little boy who used to draw pictures of passenger ships? It's good to hear your voice.'

'Where are the rest of your ships?' he asked eagerly. 'How many are coming?'

'It's only us,' she said timidly. 'The rest of the planetary guard have remained behind to, well, guard the planet. Will we do?'

'Yes, of course, every ship counts. A single laser cannon could make the difference between victory and defeat. Welcome to the fleet.' Jake flipped a few switches on his control panel. 'Attention, all ships. This is Jake Cutler. The naval warships are waiting by the Tego Nebula, and Admiral Vantard knows that we're coming, so be ready to defend yourselves. I've asked General Da Silva to lead us into battle. No one has ever raised this many ships against the Interstellar Navy, which means that we're about to make history. Whatever happens today will change the galaxy forever.'

The Independent Alliance drew nearer the Tego Nebula, which was so vast and colourful that it could be seen from other solar systems. There were five other nebula clouds in the galaxy, but none of them were as dense or ionised as this one. It was like a psychedelic storm, lit up by random streaks of lightning. Most people assumed that nothing could survive inside the Tego Nebula, which is why it had successfully concealed Altus for centuries.

Jake wondered how the other captains would react when Altus came out of hiding. He watched the cloud fill the front window like a cosmic fog. In front of it lurked a string of midnight blue shapes. Kay adjusted her scanner and swore out loud.

'I've never seen so many naval warships,' she said.

Jake swallowed hard. 'Me neither.'

It was difficult to tell where one started and another one ended. A few weeks ago, the sight of a naval warship would have sent him running. Now he was picking a fight with twenty of them, as well as thirty gunships and two hundred fighter craft. But there was no turning back. The independent colonies were depending on him, including his own planet.

'Ahoy there, Independent Alliance,' said Father Benedict over the communicator. 'This is Radio Interference with breaking news. We now know why the Interstellar Navy has gathered by the Tego Nebula. Admiral Vantard believes that there's something hidden inside the cloud. It sounds incredible, but he's convinced that the independent colonies are keeping a secret weapon in there. This was backed up further when a cargo hauler was spotted entering the nebula.'

A secret weapon? So that was why Admiral Vantard had summoned his fleet to the Tego Nebula. If one of the Space Dogs had told him there was something inside the nebula, they had managed to keep Altus out of it. Jake felt a new wave of affection for his old crew. But now the *Dark Horse* was trapped inside the cloud, along with the Altian people.

'You must retreat immediately,' warned Father Benedict. 'Admiral Vantard is taking no chances. A naval shuttle containing four mega-bombs is being launched shortly. Its robot crew will destroy whatever's inside the Tego Nebula, as well as Papa Don's illegal spaceport.'

Jake felt a stab of panic. He leapt out of his seat and ran to the window, his heart thumping.

'No,' he bellowed at the glass. 'We have to stop them.'

Kay glanced from her scanner to the display screens. 'The rest of the fleet is slowing down.'

Jake returned to his seat and activated the communicator.

'Attention, all ships. I want the fleet to keep moving, full thrust ahead.'

'Ahoy, *Divine Wind*,' said General Da Silva. 'Did you not catch the broadcast? We might get caught in the explosion.'

'It's a risk that we'll have to take,' barked Jake.

'With all due respect, my lord. Have you completely lost your mind? Why should we endanger our ships and crews to save a dust cloud and an illegal spaceport? If we're lucky, the blast will catch some of the naval warships. Is there something hidden inside the Tego Nebula?'

'Yes,' said Jake, desperate to save his friends and home planet. 'I promise to explain everything later, but we have to stop the Interstellar Navy from detonating those mega-bombs.'

Without waiting for a response, Jake opened up the throttle and the *Divine Wind* shot forward, breaking away from the other ships. He knew that a lone star frigate was no match against a naval fleet, but he had to do something.

'Are you sure about this, shipmate?' asked Kay, sounding worried for the first time.

'Just find me that shuttle,' he said.

Jake had no idea how to stop a naval shuttle carrying four mega-bombs, but it was his fault the Altian people were now at risk and he would do whatever it took to protect them.

'There are shuttles everywhere,' said Kay. 'How do we find the right one before it blows, or before our shields get shredded?'

'Perhaps you had better abandon ship,' suggested Jake. 'While you still can.'

'Don't be a guffoon,' she said, impatiently. 'Everything that I have is aboard this ship. I'm not going anywhere.'

Jake scanned the wall of naval warships. There was no way that two laser cannon could compete with over two hundred, even if the naval targeting computers were scrambled by the Tego Nebula. He was scared and he was not afraid to admit it.

'Ahoy there, *Divine Wind*,' said a deep electronic voice. 'Wait for us.'

'Vigor-8?'

'Aye, we're coming with you.'

Kay checked the scanner and her face lit up. 'It's not only *Rusty's Revenge*, others are following. The *Star Chaser*, the *Rough Diamond III*, the *Scarlet Sabre*, the *Astral Queen*, the *Half Moon* … even that travelling circus ship.'

'What about the *Sol Dorado*?' asked Jake.

Kay looked up and grinned. 'It's right behind us.'

'Ahoy, *Divine Wind*,' said General Da Silva testily. 'I thought that we were supposed to be leading this fleet together.'

Jake slowed down enough for the others to catch up and then he activated the communicator.

'Attention, all ships. Laser cannon at the ready. We need to go in hard and fast. But do not open fire on the naval shuttles, in case you hit the one carrying the mega-bombs. Keep watch for any that head towards the Tego Nebula and find a way to stop them, even if that means ramming them back into open space.' Jake switched to the intercom. 'This is it, crew. We're almost in firing range. Is everyone ready?'

'Aye,' responded Callidus. 'Capio and I have the naval fleet in our gunsights.'

'Aye,' said Kella. 'The medical bay is standing by.'

'Aye,' said Nanoo. 'Engine is operating and shields at maximum power.'

Jake turned to Kay. 'How about you?'

'Aye,' she said, with a crazed glint in her eye. 'Let's do it.'

Jake scanned the impressive row of naval warships that stretched out before them. Despite their distance, he could still make out their sharp features, which would have been identical, had some of them not already been damaged from the independent colony attacks. It was like swimming towards a shiver of sharks, but Jake was not exactly a lone defenceless fish.

With a steady hand, he activated the communicator.

'Attention, all ships. Attack! Attack! Attack!'

The bridge windows lit up as waves of laser bolts streamed past the *Divine Wind* towards the enemy fleet. At the same moment, the naval warships opened fire, creating a blinding wall of light. Jake shielded his eyes with one hand, while steering with the other.

'Use these,' shouted Kay, tossing him a pair of yellow sunglasses.

'Thanks,' he said, slipping them on and steering the *Divine Wind* through the incoming laser bolts.

'Yee-haw!' cried Kay, whose own pink sunglasses were perched awkwardly over her robotic eye.

'Keep looking for the shuttle with the mega-bombs,' said Jake, narrowly avoiding a barrel-sized laser bolt.

Kay checked her scanner. 'It could be any of them.'

'Are any shuttles heading towards the Tego Nebula?'

'Not yet, but I'll keep a watch out.'

Jake swerved to avoid another laser bolt and nearly crashed into Tark's converted racing ship, the *Half Moon*. As he swung back the other way, something nearby exploded.

'Who has been hit?'

'I think it was the travelling circus ship,' said Kay.

A group of independent colony fighters surged ahead of the *Divine Wind*, speeding towards the naval fleet in a blur of colour like a military rainbow. Jake spotted the red camouflage of Shan-Ti, the vibrant green of Libertina and the polished silver of Santanova. It was thrilling to see the treaty come to life; the colonies were united and fighting a common enemy.

In the distance, Jake spotted a series of flashes as the naval fleet took hits. He knew that the warships could withstand heavy damage – he had fought enough of them – but thanks to Nanoo, the

Independent Alliance had some pretty powerful laser cannon, which could cut through naval shields.

'It's difficult to miss with so many of them clustered together,' said Jake. 'If our lasers fail to hit one of their ships, there's a good chance that we'll hit another instead. At least our fleet is spread out enough to make us difficult targets.'

'I just hope we don't hit the shuttle carrying the …' Kay stared at the front window. 'Watch out!'

A plum-coloured fighter exploded in front of them. Jake had no time to react and the *Divine Wind* ploughed straight into its blooming debris. As they passed through the wreckage, metal fragments bombarded their shields and scraped their hull, but otherwise the star frigate emerged undamaged.

'I'm going to kiss Nanoo the next time I see him,' said Kay. 'Those shields are magnifty.'

The naval fleet was closer now and the laser bolts were becoming harder to dodge. Jake had to rely on his lightning reactions to negotiate a safe path, not daring to blink as he twisted and looped towards the enemy.

But then all of a sudden, the laser bolts stopped.

'What's going on?'

'The naval fighters are flying ahead to meet us,' said Kay, pointing at the main display. 'Not even the

Interstellar Navy would be stupid enough to shoot its own craft.'

Jake watched in horror as two hundred naval fighters descended on the Independent Alliance, like a midnight blue tidal wave.

'Hold on to your scanner,' he said. 'This is going to get rough.'

Chapter 18

Surrender

The two sides met in a spectacular exchange of laser cannon fire and explosions. Jake watched grimly as the opposing fighters clashed in a smear of colour, tearing each other apart, before any other ship could reach them. Within seconds, a third of the fighter craft had been damaged or destroyed. Moments later, the *Half Moon* charged into the fray, shortly followed by the *Sol Dorado*.

Jake aimed the *Divine Wind* at a cluster of midnight blue and accelerated hard.

'What are you doing?' exclaimed Kay. 'That has got to be at least twenty fighters.'

'The more the merrier,' said Jake adamantly.

Callidus and Capio unleashed their laser cannon. It was like disturbing a nest of angry insects. The naval fighters scattered and surrounded the *Divine Wind*, blasting it with their laser cannon. Jake took evasive action, but there were enemy craft in every direction. He rammed the nearest fighter and sent it tumbling into its neighbour, while Callidus and Capio continued to pick off targets at random.

'Shields taking much damage,' warned Nanoo over the intercom.

A huge red hull thundered past them and smashed into three naval fighters. It was the Shan-Ti warship, the *Scarlet Sabre*. Jake watched it crush the small craft, while blasting others with its laser cannon. He turned the *Divine Wind* and spotted the *Astral Queen* and *Star Chaser* also breaking through the wave of fighters.

But a lone passenger ship had become separated and it was strugging to fight off a rush of enemy craft. In the second it took Jake to realise what was happening, it was already too late. As the passenger ship attempted to escape, the naval pilots targeted its exhausts and the vessel exploded. Jake felt a thump of sorrow as its reinforced hull tore open.

After that, the naval fighters took heavy losses. All around, the Independent Alliance swatted them like flies. The remaining fighter pilots knew when to retreat and they pulled back to the Tego Nebula.

'Destroy them,' ordered Jake into the intercom. 'Before they get a chance to regroup.'

The *Divine Wind* charged after the fleeing fighters, but the moment the naval pilots were clear, the warships resumed their bombardment. This time, the naval laser cannon concentrated their fire on two or three ships, which was instantly effective.

Kay cursed and thumped the scanner. 'We've lost the *Astral Queen*.'

Jake tried not to think about Captain Lee Quinn and his crew. There would be time to honour the dead later.

'Here they come,' he said, as the naval warships flew out to meet them. 'Where is that shuttle?'

'I don't know ... Wait a moment.' Kay leant closer to the scanner and fiddled with her robotic eye. 'There's a lone shuttle breaking away from the naval fleet. It's heading straight for the Tego Nebula.'

The most epic space battle in the history of the seven solar systems was taking place, but it would have to wait. In a matter of minutes, the naval shuttle would enter the Tego Nebula and release its four mega-bombs. Jake had to stop that shuttle, before it destroyed Altus and Papa Don's.

'The *Star Chaser* has damaged a naval warship,' reported Kay excitedly. 'And the salvage trawlers are battling a group of gunships. That *Rough Diamond III* is a real scrapper.'

'Good,' said Jake. 'But if we don't stop that shuttle, both sides will be caught in the blast. We have to break through the naval fleet. Can you find me a gap in their defences?'

Kay searched her display. 'There isn't one, those naval warships are keeping their formation tight.'

'There's only one thing for it,' said Jake grimly. 'We're going to have to make a gap.'

'And how are we going to do that?'

Jake activated the communicator. 'Ahoy, *Sol Dorado*. I need a favour.'

General Da Silva listened while Jake explained his plan.

'Leave it to me,' said the general. 'I'll gather a few of our ships and we'll smash our way through that blockade.'

Jake eased off the thrusters and waited for the *Sol Dorado* to make its move. His fingers drummed the control panel impatiently as he watched the shuttle edge closer to the nebula cloud.

'Blast!' growled Kay, thumping her scanner.

'Are you OK?' asked Jake.

'No,' she said. 'This useless thing keeps flickering.'

'I'm not surprised, the Tego Nebula affects most modern devices. It's probably why the naval gunners keep missing our ships. I had better warn the others.'

Jake informed the rest of the crew about the increasing effects of the nebula static. In response, Callidus and Capio switched off their targeting computers so they could aim manually.

Seconds later, the *Sol Dorado* pulled ahead of the fleet as planned, flanked by the *Scarlet Sabre* and the *Half Moon*. Jake followed behind, gathering pace as they charged. His eyes kept darting back to the display. The naval shuttle was less than a minute from the Tego Nebula.

'My dad would have loved this,' said Kay, her good eye soaking up the enemy barricade.

All four ships remained in formation, only deviating from their course to dodge laser bolts or naval fighters. Other crews helped by blasting wreckage out of their path. General Da Silva gave the order to target a single naval warship.

BOOM!

A lucky shot caught the *Divine Wind*. Its shields held, but Jake had to fight to regain control as the star frigate tumbled off course.

BOOM!

BOOM!

Two more laser bolts pounded the shields and Jake was forced to break formation. He sent the *Divine Wind* into a spin to avoid further hits, but by the time he pulled up, they had fallen behind. The other three ships were concentrating their laser cannon on a single naval warship. It crumbled like a washed out sandcastle and exploded, creating a hole in the enemy defences.

'Hurry, Jake,' urged Kay.

'I know,' he said, opening the throttle to maximum. 'Hold on.'

Using every drop of thrust, the *Divine Wind* accelerated towards the gap. The other three ships had done their part and were turning back to rejoin the fleet.

'Jake,' pressed Kay.

The surrounding naval warships were already starting to close the gap. Jake focused on the narrowing space and gripped the controls.

'This is going to be tight,' he warned.

Laser bolts skimmed the electronic shields, as the *Divine Wind* raced towards the gap. Callidus and Capio did their best to blast debris out of the way, but Jake was still forced to fly through metal shards and broken glass, which sparkled like crystals as they streamed past the windows.

'We'll never fit,' said Kay.

'Yes, we will,' insisted Jake.

BOOM!

At the last second, a laser bolt hit the hull and Jake felt the *Divine Wind* twist awkwardly. It was too late to pull away, so he aimed the nose of the ship at the closing gap and braced for impact.

CRASH!

The *Divine Wind* rebounded off a warship hull with a thunderous scraping sound, but the star frigate kept moving. It squeezed through the gap and popped out the other side.

'You did it,' cheered Kay. 'We're behind enemy lines.'

But there was no time to celebrate.

'Where's that shuttle?' asked Jake, frantically.

'There,' she said, pointing at the window.

Jake followed her finger and saw the small craft on the edge of the Tego Nebula. He activated the intercom, which rustled loudly with static.

'Callidus, Capio, stop that shuttle!'

'How?' replied the fortune seeker. 'If we target its exhausts from this distance, we might hit the mega-bombs.'

'If you don't try, the bombs will definitely explode,' said Jake. 'Take the shot.'

Callidus and Capio opened fire on the naval shuttle, but it was too late. Jake watched helplessly as the small craft entered the nebula cloud and melted from view.

'Now what?' asked Kay.

'We go after it,' said Jake determinedly.

'Are you insane? We'll never find it in that foul fog.'

'We have to try.' Jake could hear the desperation in his own voice. 'We have to stop them.'

'I'm sorry,' she said, 'but it could take us days to find the shuttle in there and those mega-bombs are going to explode at any second.'

The *Divine Wind* reached the edge of the swirling nebula and Jake had to swerve to avoid a bolt of lightning, which lashed out at them like a giant whip. He stared at the immense cloud in a state of shock. It was as though the natural protector of his own planet had turned against him.

'What about my people?' he said, his voice shaking. 'And the Space Dogs?'

Kay shook her head solemnly. 'It's too late, shipmate. We tried our best, but now we've got to get out of here, before we get caught in the blast.'

Jake pictured the naval robots activating the mega-bombs and he felt sick. Kay was right, there was no way to stop the shuttle now. All they could do was stay alive long enough to avenge Altus and save the other colonies. He seemed to stir from a trance and remember the battle being fought behind them.

'I'm going to kill those wretchards,' he roared, seizing the controls. 'I'm going to destroy every last one of them.'

The *Divine Wind* swung back towards the naval warships, which were now in close combat with the Independent Alliance. Laser bolts and explosions lit up the stars as the two fleets bombarded each other. Jake's anger seemed to feed off the carnage. The *Divine Wind* soared up behind the Interstellar Navy and opened fire, catching the naval gunners off guard. Jake watched with grim satisfaction as a midnight blue hull tore apart, followed by another.

'Come on!' cried Kay. 'We have to get to a safe distance. The explosion is going to be epic.'

'The explosion?' Jake was too angry to think straight, but something wasn't right. He turned in his seat and stared at the Tego Nebula through the side window. 'It should have happened by now. What are the robots waiting for?'

'I ... I don't know.'

Had something gone wrong? Jake bit back his rage and activated the communicator.

'Father Benedict, can you hear me?' he said. 'I need to know what happened to the naval shuttle that entered the Tego Nebula. Can you help?'

There was an agonising silence that lasted for thirty seconds … a minute … two minutes … until a familiar voice filled the speakers.

'Ahoy there, Independent Alliance,' said the cyber-abbot. 'It appears that the mega-bombs did not detonate as expected. No one seems to know what happened to the naval shuttle. Admiral Vantard is furious and he wants to send in a warship to find out, but some of the naval captains are talking about surrender.'

Jake's spirits lifted. Surrender? He had come to the seventh solar system prepared to lose everything, including his life. Did he dare to hope for victory? Another two naval warships exploded and Jake had a sudden inspiration. He flipped a switch on the communicator and put on his most commanding voice.

'Ahoy, *ISS Magnificent*,' he said. 'This is Jake Cutler, ruler of Altus and leader of the Independent Alliance. Your fleet has suffered heavy losses. Surrender now and I will spare your remaining crews.'

'Ahoy, Kid Cutler,' snarled Admiral Vantard. 'We do not negotiate with space pirates. You may have the advantage, but this battle is far from over.'

'Surrender now,' said Jake, darkly, 'or I will release my secret weapon from the nebula.'

This had the effect that Jake had intended. The communicator fell silent and he knew that he had the admiral worried. But would his ruse be convincing enough to end the battle, or would Vantard call his bluff?

Chapter 19

Resurrection

The naval warships ceased fire and clustered together. Jake instructed the Independent Alliance to 'cool their cannon' and surround the enemy. As they carried out his orders, he calculated the damage sustained by each side. There were twelve Independent Alliance ships remaining, supported by twenty fighter craft, but there were only eight naval vessels. His fleet had fared better than he could have ever hoped.

Jake imagined the naval captains insisting that Admiral Vantard surrender for the sake of their crews. This was it, he could sense the moment. Any second now, the Interstellar Navy would power down their laser cannon, close their gun ports and give up their ships. Jake shivered with excitement as he awaited their response.

'That's funny,' said Kay, thumping her scanner. 'My screen cleared for a second and I could have sworn that I saw something ... but it can't have been ... I must have imagined it.'

'Imagined what?' asked Jake, not taking his eyes off the communicator.

Kay looked up and swore out loud, before staggering away from the window. 'That!'

Jake turned and saw something outside that no longer belonged in the seven solar systems. He blinked his purple implants in case they were playing tricks on him. Scargus and Manik had warned him about space mirages, which occur when crews spend too much time staring at the stars, but this was no illusion.

'That's impossible,' he muttered. 'It was destroyed.'

'It's a ghost ship,' said Kay, her voice verging on hysterical.

Jake felt a sharp chill at the sight of a naval super-destroyer, its massive hull scarred with tentacle marks and laser cannon damage.

There were no ghosts in space, but how else could they be looking at the *ISS Colossus*?

Time seemed to slow as the giant warship cast its shadow over the Independent Alliance. It was easily the largest vessel in the galaxy. The last time that Jake had seen the super-destroyer, it had been sucked inside a black hole on the edge of the seventh solar system. How could it have survived? Nothing ever came back out of a black hole ... until now.

Callidus and Capio rushed on to the bridge, closely followed by Kella and Nanoo.

'Jake –' uttered Kella.

'I know.'

Callidus stared at the display. 'I wouldn't have believed it, if I hadn't seen it with my own eyes.'

The ISS Colossus stopped moving.

'What it doing?' asked Nanoo.

'Picking its target,' said Jake, noticing the open gun ports.

The solar tide had turned. A moment ago the Independent Alliance had been on the verge of victory, but the arrival of the ISS Colossus had changed everything.

Jake was transfixed by the super-destroyer as it turned slowly towards them. A few of its lights still flickered from the damage it had sustained months before.

'Here we go again!' exclaimed Capio.

'Ahoy, Divine Wind.' General Da Silva sounded shaken. 'What are your orders, my lord?'

Before Jake could respond, a single ship flew out towards the ISS Colossus, firing its laser cannon. The converted space tug looked like a tiny toy in the shadow of the super-destroyer.

'What is Vigor-8 doing?' gasped Kella.

'That robot has guts,' said Kay. 'Not even I would be crazy enough to take on the *ISS Colossus*.'

Jake grabbed the communicator. 'Ahoy, *Rusty's Revenge*. Break off your attack immediately, that's an order.'

There was no way of knowing if the robot crew had heard. A flurry of laser bolts engulfed *Rusty's Revenge* and ripped apart its hull. Jake watched helplessly as the old space tug disintegrated before his eyes. The Hacker Jackers may have been machines, but as far as he was concerned, they had been his friends.

'My lord?' pressed General Da Silva, more urgently.

'Hold fire,' ordered Jake, doing his best to control his shock. 'Nobody move a rivet.'

The entire fleet obeyed except for a swamp brown gunship from Ho Dan, which broke ranks and fled. Kay tracked it on the scanner as it gathered speed, but Jake knew that it could not outrun a naval laser cannon. Several shots from the *ISS Colossus* caught the gunship and it exploded. None of the other crews tried to escape after that.

'Ahoy, *Divine Wind*,' said a cold, sour voice. 'Did you miss me?'

Until that moment, Jake had wondered if the *ISS Colossus* had been real, or if another ship had been built to look like it, but there was no mistaking the scratchy tones of Admiral Algor Nex. The voice triggered a rush of painful memories: the monastery attack on Remota that killed Father Pius, the service port raid that killed Amicus Kent, and the battle of the black hole that nearly killed them all.

'Ahoy, *ISS Colossus*,' said Jake, determined to put on a brave front. 'We preferred it when you were dead.'

Admiral Nex laughed venomously. 'It will take more than a black hole to stop this ship, Kid Cutler. We were trapped in that wretched place for months, working in complete darkness and suffering from the crushing gravity. But now we're back and we want revenge.'

The other naval warships resumed battle formation, but they made no attempt to fire. Admiral Vantard and his captains were probably just as surprised to see the *ISS Colossus* return.

'Kill me and you'll never find Altus,' said Jake, thinking quickly.

'Nice try,' sneered Admiral Nex. 'But your planet can wait. The only thing that kept me going the last few months was the thought of killing you.'

It was over. Jake couldn't talk his way out of this one and there was no point offering their surrender.

With a crushing realisation, he knew that it was the end of the Independent Alliance. Once the *ISS Colossus* opened fire, the other naval warships would join in the attack.

'So what are you waiting for?' shouted Jake in frustration. 'Take your best shot.'

'Patience, young Cutler,' taunted Admiral Nex. 'I have a parting gift for you.'

The communicator fell silent.

'What did he mean by that?' asked Capio nervously.

'I don't know,' said Callidus. 'But nothing good has ever come out of that ship.'

'Hey,' shouted Kay. 'It has fired something.'

'A laser cannon?' Jake checked the display.

'No, it looks like an escape pod.'

Jake located the tiny capsule shooting towards them, like a spinning cannonball. What was Admiral Nex playing at?

'It probably contains a mega-bomb,' groaned Capio.

'I don't think it's big enough,' reasoned Jake.

'There's only one way to find out what's inside that escape pod,' said Callidus. 'And that's to open it.'

Jake grabbed the controls and matched the capsule's trajectory.

'Kella, I want you to seal the inner hatch and lower the loading ramp,' he instructed. 'I'm going to catch the escape pod in the cargo hold.'

The *Divine Wind* turned and accelerated away from the *ISS Colossus*, while Kella made her way downstairs. Jake was confident that Admiral Nex would not open fire until his gift had been delivered.

'The inner door is sealed and the ramp is open,' reported Kella over the intercom.

Jake lined up the star frigate and allowed the escape pod to creep up behind them, watching it edge nearer on the display.

'That's it,' said Callidus. 'A little slower, steady, steady.'

Jake felt the ship lurch as the escape pod hit the loading ramp and rolled into the cargo hold. He turned the *Divine Wind* back to face the *ISS Colossus* and cut the thrusters.

The entire crew charged down to the cargo hold, where Kella was waiting. Callidus and Kay drew their laser pistols as they waited for the loading ramp to close. The escape pod sat motionless, steam hissing from a vent on its circular hatch.

'I still reckon it's a trap,' moaned Capio.

Jake unsheathed his cutlass. 'Let's find out.'

The inner hatch opened and the six of them surrounded the escape pod, weapons at the ready. Jake watched it expectantly, as though it were a giant egg waiting to hatch. What was supposed to happen next? His heart beat harder as he stepped closer and listened to sounds of movement inside.

Clang!

Without warning, the circular hatch popped open and a figure emerged, shielding his eyes from the light.

'It's a cyber-monk,' said Capio.

'It's a cyber-abbot,' corrected Callidus.

'It's Father Pius,' said Jake, dropping his cutlass at the sight of the man who had raised him.

No one spoke as the old man clambered out of the escape pod on unsteady legs. He looked pale and weary, but it was definitely Father Pius, the cyber-abbot who had cared for Jake. In his wrinkled hand, he clutched an official-looking package.

'How can this be?' Jake plunged his fingers into his thick brown hair. 'What are you doing here, father? I thought you were dead.'

The cyber-abbot twisted around and squinted at him with abnormally wide pupils. 'Jake?'

Kella stepped forward to help Father Pius, but Callidus pulled her back.

'Hold on,' he said. 'It could be a trick. That package might be dangerous.'

Jake's mind raced with questions: How had the cyber-abbot survived the monastery attack? What was he doing aboard the *ISS Colossus*? Had he been inside the black hole this whole time? But as Jake looked at the frail old man, he realised that none of that mattered at that moment, when they were so close to the end. After a short pause, he asked the question that seemed most pressing.

'What's that in your hands?'

Father Pius leant against the escape pod. He was clearly scared and disoriented. With a shaking hand, he held out the package and spoke in a hoarse voice. 'Admiral Nex says that it would be fitting for you to die wearing this.'

Jake took the package and opened it.

'What is it?' asked Kella.

Jake reached inside and pulled out a polished gold object covered in strange markings. He turned it in his hands to discover a space pirate emblem and a circle containing three crystals: a diamond, a ruby and an emerald.

'It's the crown of Altus.'

Jake stared at it in wonder. At last, he had the three unique items that had been passed down to each ruler of Altus: the pendant, the sword and the crown. He had only seen them united in photos, worn by his ancestors, but this was the first time that he'd possessed them all. His thumb stroked the pirate emblem engraved on the heavy crown and its significance coursed through his body. It had been worn by the first pirate king and ruler of Altus, Captain Alyus Don.

Kay whistled appreciatively. 'Nice crown!'

The others gathered around him to admire the object. Jake caught sight of something inside the rim. He turned the crown in his hands to discover two strange sockets, like the ports on a computer. Why were they so familiar?

'What is it?' asked Callidus.

Jake pushed the crown back inside the package. 'Nothing. It can wait. We need to get back to the battle.'

'Yes,' agreed Nanoo. 'Admiral Nex not hold fire forever.'

Father Pius started at the sight of the Novu boy.

'It's OK,' said Jake. 'This is my friend, Nanoo. He's from a planet called Taan-Centaur in a distant galaxy. Next to him is Kella, our ship's medic. The pink-haired pirate is Kay. You know Callidus, and the other man is his companion, Capio.'

Father Pius bowed his head politely. 'Good to meet you.'

'We've delayed long enough,' said Jake, darkly. 'It's time to face Admiral Nex.'

Chapter 20

Reinforcements

The crew filed from the cargo hold and Father Pius limped after them.

'Let me help you, father,' offered Jake.

'Thank you,' said the cyber-abbot, taking his hand. 'Are we going to fight?'

Jake nodded. 'We're preparing for the fight of our lives.'

Admiral Nex had intended for the crown to shock and discourage Jake, but instead it had inspired the exact opposite effect. The crown had given Jake a renewed sense of energy and purpose. It had reminded him of his home planet and how he needed to win this battle for the sake of his people.

The pair of them reached the bridge and Jake took his seat at the controls. After a quick glance at the *ISS Colossus*, he activated the communicator.

'Ahoy, *Sol Dorado*. Are you there, General Da Silva?'

'Ahoy, *Divine Wind*. Where the ruddy guff have you been? We've been trying to get hold of you.

I don't think we can win this fight. We'll need the whole fleet to fight that super-destroyer, never mind the rest of those naval warships.'

'Surrender is not an option,' said Jake firmly. 'If we close our gun ports, the Interstellar Navy will destroy us anyway. I want the fleet to target the *ISS Colossus* and wait for my lead. If we're going to die, we're going to take that super-destroyer with us, so it can't be used against the independent colonies.'

There was a sharp intake of breath. 'Aye, my lord.'

Jake changed the channel.

'Ahoy, *ISS Colossus*,' he said. 'Thank you for the gift, Admiral Nex. It means more than you could possibly know.'

A cruel laugh filled the speakers. 'Ahoy, *Divine Wind*. I'm surprised it fits.'

'The crown?' Jake paused for effect. 'I'm sure that it will fit my dad perfectly.'

'Your father? Andras Cutler is dead.'

'No more than you.'

Jake had stalled long enough. He stole a brief glance at his friends, who had gathered behind him. His face must have told them what he was planning to do.

Father Pius smiled kindly. 'Do what you think is right.'

223

Kay shrugged. 'It was fun while it lasted, shipmate.'

Kella stood tall. 'No one messes with a space-jacker.'

Nanoo let out a shrill Novu war cry. 'We in this together, until the end.'

Jake nodded and turned back to the communicator.

'Attention, all ships, this is Jake Cutler. In the name of independence, I order you … I beg of you … attack!'

The remaining vessels swarmed around the *ISS Colossus*, blasting its shields at close range. A few seconds later, the other naval warships opened fire. Jake tested his pilot skills to their limit, weaving around the enemy craft and dodging their laser bolts, while Callidus and Capio unleashed the laser cannon.

'We've lost two more ships,' reported Kay grimly.

Jake caught sight of a Libertina fighter crashing into the *ISS Colossus*. Its shell crumpled like an insect under a gravity boot. The shields rippled on impact, but held as the super-destroyer turned to pursue the *Divine Wind*.

'We're not done yet,' insisted Jake, using the star frigate's speed to avoid being targeted, but their path was blocked by the *ISS Magnificent*.

The speakers crackled and hissed.

'Ahoy, *Divine Wind*,' said Admiral Vantard. 'You almost had us, Kid Cutler, before the *ISS Colossus* showed up. But playtime is over. There is no secret weapon inside that nebula, otherwise you would have used it by now. Any last words, before we blow you to stardust?'

'I told you the truth about the *ISS Colossus*,' shouted Jake into the communicator. 'No one murdered Admiral Nex.'

'None of that matters now,' said Admiral Vantard. 'Not since you destroyed half of my fleet. Space Dog? You're more like a mad dog that needs putting down. In the name of the United Worlds, prepare to die.'

'You first!'

'Wait … What's that?'

'Jake,' called Kay, watching her scanner. 'There's something coming out of the Tego Nebula.'

It took him a moment to register what she had said. He turned to his flickering display screen and searched for signs of movement. Was it the missing naval shuttle? Had the robots lost their way and were they now returning with the four megabombs? A cluster of tiny shapes burst from the multicoloured cloud, led by an old cargo hauler with a plump hull.

'It's the *Dark Horse*!' cheered Jake, as he prepared to attack the *ISS Magnificent*.

'What's a horse doing inside the Tego Nebula?' asked Father Pius.

'The *Dark Horse* is the most wanted pirate ship in the galaxy,' explained Jake, keeping an eye on the *ISS Magnificent* and *ISS Colossus*. 'But it's on our side and it has brought the Altian planetary guard.'

Altus had a small fleet of old-fashioned ships, which were kept in case the planet was ever discovered. These ships only had basic shields and weapons, but at that moment, the Independent Alliance needed all the help it could get.

'Ahoy, *Divine Wind*,' croaked Granny Leatherhead, her voice crackling with static. 'Sorry we're late. The Protectorate took a bit of convincing, but General Kent and I made them see reason in the end. I'm sure that someone will let them out of their basement eventually … Wait a minute … Shoot me sideways, is that the *ISS Colossus*?'

'I'll explain later,' said Jake, aware that the super-destroyer was now directly behind the *Divine Wind* and preparing to fire. 'It's good to see you.'

'Is that it?' scoffed Admiral Vantard from the *ISS Magnificent*. 'Is that your secret weapon? An old cargo hauler and a collection of antique ships?'

'It's not only them,' said Kay excitedly. 'There's another ship launching from Papa Don's. It's the *Lost Soul*.'

'Captain James Hawker?'

Jake spotted the large black cruiser, which was the second most wanted ship in the galaxy. The last time he had encountered the *Lost Soul*, their ships had been on opposing sides.

'Ahoy, *Divine Wind*,' said a coarse voice. 'Is there room for an old spacejacker and his crew?'

Jake didn't trust Captain Hawker, but at that moment he had nothing to lose. 'Ahoy, *Lost Soul*. Welcome to the war.'

Admiral Nex joined in the discussion. His callous voice trickled through the speakers like poison.

'A couple of old pirate ships and a handful of vintage craft won't save you, Jake Cutler,' he said nastily. 'Where did you find them? In a museum? It's a pity you don't have anything more advanced –'

'Wait a moment, Algor,' interrupted Admiral Vantard. 'Are those Altian vessels?'

'No,' lied Jake, but his desperate tone gave him away.

'Yes!' roared Admiral Nex, unable to control himself. 'I recognise the symbol on their hulls. So that's where Altus has been hiding. It's inside the wretched Tego Nebula.'

While the admirals were distracted, Jake quickly surveyed the space battle and spotted the *Sol Dorado*, the *Scarlet Sabre*, the *Star Chaser* and the *Half Moon* blasting the *ISS Colossus*. The *Dark Horse* and the *Lost Soul* were fighting side by side, attacking naval warships with equal ferocity, while the Altian craft took on the naval fighters. He had never witnessed such courage and determination, but victory still seemed impossible.

Whatever happened, Jake knew that the *Divine Wind* would not survive to see the end. The battered old star frigate was caught between the *ISS Colossus* and *ISS Magnificent*. All that was left for him to do was to decide how best to die.

'What are you doing?' asked Kella.

'I'm turning the *Divine Wind* about to face the *ISS Colossus*,' said Jake. 'As much as I would like to blast the dashing smile off Admiral Vantard's face, we have to stop that super-destroyer, whatever it takes.'

'But how we do that?' asked Nanoo.

'Leave it to me.' Jake found himself surprisingly calm and focused. 'If I can take out the *ISS Colossus*, the others might stand a chance against the rest of the naval warships. Get yourselves to the escape pod in the cargo hold.'

'I'm not going anywhere,' said Kay. 'I would rather die aboard my ship, than cowering inside a naval escape pod.'

'But –'

'And the same goes for the rest of us,' said Kella.

'Aye to that,' agreed Nanoo.

Jake looked imploringly at Father Pius.

'There's not enough time for me to get to the cargo hold anyway,' said the cyber-abbot, with a weak smile.

'It has been great knowing you, shipmates,' said Jake, turning back to his controls. 'I'm sorry it has to end this way.'

The enormous *ISS Colossus* filled the front window. Jake knew that Callidus and Capio were struggling to penetrate its shields, but perhaps the *Divine Wind* itself was tough enough to break through and pierce its hull.

'Jake, what's going on?' asked Callidus over the intercom.

'We're going to ram the *ISS Colossus*. If you hurry, you and Capio can make it to the escape pod.'

'We're not leaving you,' said Callidus. 'If nothing else, we can help to weaken its shields as we draw near.'

Jake had no time to argue. He squeezed the thrusters and the *Divine Wind* surged forward, accelerating hard towards the naval super-destroyer for its final assault.

The *ISS Colossus* opened fire and the windows of the *Divine Wind* filled with light. It was so bright that Jake was sure the star frigate had been destroyed. He instinctively shielded his eyes, but there was no explosion or shattering of glass.

'I can't see,' said Father Pius. 'It's blinding.'

'Were we hit?' asked Kella.

'Are we dead?' wondered Kay.

'It not laser bolt,' said Nanoo excitedly. 'It my Uncle Morc.'

The light dimmed to reveal something that Jake would never forget. In front of them, the *ISS Colossus* sat motionless, like a wreck. Its lights were out, its shields were down and its laser cannon were silent. The only reason that Jake could still see the super-destroyer was because of the glow radiating from the surrounding spacecraft.

His jaw dropped at the sight of three giant vessels, each one triple the size of the *ISS Colossus*.

'Are those Novu warships?' Jake eased off the thrusters and let the star frigate drift. 'Nanoo, when you sent your message home, did you mention the galactic war by any chance?'

'Yes, how you know?'

Jake laughed nervously. 'Just a guess.'

As they watched in amazement, two of the naval fighters opened fire on the Novu warships. There was another flash of light and the fighters were rendered powerless. The remaining naval vessels held their laser cannon.

'How did they do that?' asked Father Pius.

'It Novu technology,' said Nanoo proudly. 'We not have wars on Taan-Centaur, but we ready in case of danger. My Uncle Morc is commander of Novu fleet. He not hurt naval crews, only melt engines and disable weapons.'

An eerie silence followed. Where there had been a raging battle moments ago, not a single laser bolt fired now.

'It's over,' whispered Kella. 'The Battle of the Tego Nebula is over.'

A loud noise clicked through the speakers, followed by a high-pitched whistling.

'What is that?' asked Father Pius.

'It my language.' Nanoo rushed over to the communicator and spoke into the microphone with his own mixture of clicks and whistles. 'I tell my Uncle Morc that I am not harmed.'

The speakers filled with a more urgent tapping noise.

'What did he say?' asked Jake.

Nanoo did not answer straight away. The young Novu boy stared at the speaker for a moment before translating.

'He say it time for me to go home.'

Chapter 21

Uncle Morc

'Go?' Kella shook her head. 'But you can't go yet.'

'We still need your help,' said Jake. 'The battle might be over, but not the war. We would be unbeatable with those Novu warships.'

Nanoo spoke into the communicator once more. 'Uncle Morc say that Novu cannot fight your war. He only here to save me.'

'But the Independent Alliance has sustained heavy losses,' protested Jake. 'How can we fight the rest of the Interstellar Navy and take down the Interstellar Government with only a dozen ships?'

Nanoo shrugged. It was out of his hands.

'Jake,' interrupted Kay. 'A naval gunship has just blasted its way out of the *ISS Colossus*. It looks as though Admiral Nex is making a run for it.'

Jake checked the display screen and spotted a jagged hole on the side of the super-destroyer. Not far away, a lone naval gunship was speeding towards the sixth solar system. The Novu weapon must have only disabled the warship engine. As he watched, several more gunships and fighter craft squeezed out of the hole, before heading off in different directions.

'We have to go after Nex,' said Jake, 'before he can fetch reinforcements or return to Naval Command.'

'How do we know which is his ship?' Father Pius gestured to the window. 'Besides, I doubt that the Novu will let us leave here with Nanoo still aboard.'

'The other naval warships are moving,' said Kella. 'But they're not running. It looks as though they're creating a blockade to stop us following the escaping craft.'

Anger and frustration boiled inside Jake. Why had the Novu not disabled the other naval warships? Did they only attack those who posed a direct threat to Nanoo? Jake changed the channel on his communicator.

'Ahoy, *ISS Magnificent*. This is Jake Cutler. I order you to surrender and move your ships out of our way immediately. Do you hear me, Admiral Vantard?'

'Ahoy, *Divine Wind*. I'm sorry, Kid Cutler, but I cannot do that. My orders are to remain in position until Admiral Nex is clear.'

'Move now, or be destroyed.'

'I have my orders.'

'Do you want to die?' Jake was furious. 'Is that twisted old man worth the lives of your crews?'

There was a brief pause before Admiral Vantard responded.

'No,' he said grudgingly. 'I know when I'm beaten and I will surrender for the sake of my crew. We've given Admiral Nex a good head start. I doubt that your warships will catch him now.'

Jake changed channels. 'Attention, all ships. Admiral Vantard has surrendered. Prepare to go after Admiral Nex.'

'Ahoy, *Divine Wind*,' said General Da Silva. 'I'm sorry, my lord, but we cannot leave yet. The fleet has just fought the biggest space battle in history. We have wounded crews to heal, damaged ships to repair and naval prisoners to arrest.'

'And I need to get my eyes checked,' commented Baden Scott. 'For a moment there, I thought that I saw a naval super-destroyer back from the dead, a load of spacecraft from Altus and three alien warships!'

Jake could no longer see the escaping gunships and fighters. Admiral Nex was getting away and there was nothing he could do to stop him. Would the admiral find more Gork warships in the sixth solar system, or would he crawl straight back to Naval Command in the first solar system?

'We can use the *Dark Horse*,' said Jake. 'It's fast enough to catch a naval gunship and it's not too damaged. I'm sure the Space Dogs won't mind.'

'It's too late.' Kay looked up from her scanner. 'I've lost them. The gunships and fighters have gone out of range.'

'Blast it!' shouted Jake. 'We'll never find him now.'

'Yes, we will,' said Kella. 'We'll find that wretchard, even if we have to search every planet for him.'

'With only a dozen ships?'

The speakers crackled and popped.

'Ahoy there, Independent Alliance, this is Radio Interference,' said Father Benedict cheerily. 'I wanted to be the first to congratulate you on your victory. It was hard to follow the battle with the interference from the Tego Nebula, but we got the general gist.'

'Thanks,' replied Jake miserably. 'We won the battle, but we lost Admiral Nex and we gave away the location of Altus. If we're going to win this war, we're going to need more ships.'

Jake set to work arresting Admiral Vantard and his naval crews. With help from General Da Silva, Captain Swan and Captain Harley, they locked the prisoners inside their own cells and took control of their ships. Kay joked that they were all spacejackers now, which General Da Silva did not find funny. Volunteer skeleton crews were left to pilot the naval warships to the nearest spaceport, where the prisoners would be held until after the war. Jake had considered using the warships in battle, but it would be far too confusing and his fleet might end up killing one of its own crews by mistake.

Nanoo stayed long enough to help with the essential repairs, before he gathered his things. Jake got the impression that Nanoo was putting off the moment when he would have to say goodbye. But when the nearest Novu warship descended and swallowed the *Divine Wind* into its glowing hangar deck, Jake knew that the time had come.

Nanoo met them by the airlock with his bag of clothes and alien gadgets.

'My Uncle Morc waiting,' he said, glumly. 'But I not sure I want to go.'

'Don't you miss your home?' asked Kella.

'Yes, I miss Taan-Centaur, very much,' said Nanoo. 'But it not be the same without parents. I have new family now, here in this galaxy.'

The Novu boy stared anxiously at the airlock door.

'Would you like us to come with you?' asked Jake.

Nanoo looked surprised. 'You come to Taan-Centaur?'

'No,' said Jake quickly. 'I meant come with you to see your Uncle Morc. Don't get me wrong, I would love to see your home planet one day, but not while the independent colonies need our help.'

Nanoo nodded and the three of them stepped into the airlock. Kella opened the outer door and they were greeted by a warm light.

If Jake had thought naval warships were bright and clean, they were nothing compared with a Novu vessel. He had half expected to see dark and dusty corridors, like the wreck from which he had rescued Nanoo, but this ship was glowing with life.

'Come,' said Nanoo, leading the way.

Jake and Kella followed him through the giant hangar deck, which contained several Novu craft. The floor was not made of metal, but a strange supple substance, like rubber or putty. A gentle wind howled around them and Jake could smell chemicals, possibly alien fuel cells or engine oil.

As they reached a set of double doors, they were greeted by two Novu shipmates, who towered over them. Their uniforms were made out of a stretchy skin-like material and they carried peculiar handheld devices, which were most likely weapons.

The two shipmates spoke to Nanoo in a mixture of loud clicks and whistles. Jake did not understand a word, but their tone and body language was clear. He guessed that they wanted to know why Nanoo had brought two humans with him.

'My Uncle Morc on bridge,' said Nanoo. 'Kanaak and Mindeeg take us to him.'

A special transport pod carried them up to the top deck. When Jake had lived on Remota, he would have given anything to be aboard a spacecraft. Now, he found himself standing on the bridge of an alien warship. His eyes soaked up the sleek design with its oval windows and holographic displays. The glowing walls appeared semi-transparent and Jake could see faint stars through them. In front of him, Novu shipmates had plunged their arms inside rubbery slots on the walls, as though they were plugged into the warship's controls.

'Ahoy,' said a deep Novu accent, before it slipped into clicks and whistles.

A Novu officer approached them, who looked similar to Nanoo, except older, with gaunt features and a bluish tint to his lilac skin. Jake noticed several markings on his face, like tattoos or serial numbers. It had to be Uncle Morc.

The Novu general stooped down to examine Jake and Kella, before letting out a low whistle.

'He say thank you for looking after me,' translated Nanoo.

'Erm, no problem,' said Jake.

Kella smiled at Uncle Morc. 'It's a pleasure to meet you.'

'It pleasure,' repeated the Novu general.

'Are you sure he can't help us?' asked Jake. 'We would easily win the war with this technology.'

Nanoo spoke with his uncle for several long minutes, while making frantic gestures to the window and his friends. When he had finished, Uncle Morc reluctantly nodded.

'Does that mean he's going to help?' asked Jake.

'No,' said Nanoo. 'But I will.'

Kella frowned. 'I don't understand.'

'My uncle not able to interfere in human war, so he let me stay instead. We Novu can make one request in the name of our dead, it is tradition. I ask to stay here to finish my parents' work. It mean that I can help you first.'

'But this is your chance to go home,' said Jake.

'It OK, my uncle give me exploration ship with Novu engine and long-distance communicator. I can go home when parents' work complete.'

Jake broke into a broad grin. His friend was staying. It would have been nice to have a Novu warship on their side, but if that wasn't possible, the next best thing was Nanoo. His inventions had already saved their lives on numerous occasions. Jake looked forward to seeing what Nanoo could do with a Novu exploration ship.

'Let's get out of here,' whispered Jake. 'Before your uncle changes his mind.'

The three of them bowed to Uncle Morc and raced back to the hangar deck, where Nanoo assured Jake and Kella that he could fly the Novu exploration ship on his own. Jake and Kella returned to the *Divine Wind* to find Callidus, Capio, Kay and Father Pius waiting for them on the bridge.

'We've checked the entire ship,' said Callidus. 'This star frigate has seen better days, but it's holding together.'

Jake looked at the tatty walls around them. 'As long as we can make it to the first solar system.'

Kay hoisted her thumb at the window. 'You've got a message from Papa Don. Old crystal features contacted us while you were out. He says congratulations on the battle, it was most entertaining. Apparently, his spaceport made a load of money from people betting against you. He still wants his sword back, but he says that you can keep it for now, seeing as you're both descendants of the same pirate king.'

'He should be thanking us for saving his space mafia skin,' huffed Kella. 'All that power and he lets others risk their lives.'

'While we're on the subject,' said Kay. 'It looks as though Captain Hawker has had enough of the war. His ship has skulked back to Papa Don's.'

'There's a surprise,' snorted Kella. 'But at least he got his hands dirty when it counted.'

Jake climbed into the pilot's seat and spotted his handheld computer resting on the control panel. He picked up the device and stared at it for a moment, his eyes scanning its familiar dents and scratches.

'Here,' he said, passing it to Father Pius. 'This belongs to you. I'm sorry about the damage.'

The cyber-abbot took the handheld computer and blinked at it in astonishment. He turned the device over in his hands and used his skull implants to connect with it. The special implants enabled cyber-monks to control computers with their thoughts.

'There are some files missing,' he said.

'Father Benedict removed your research notes on Shan-Ti,' explained Jake. 'But I don't think he found as much information as he hoped.'

Jake could have sworn that he saw the cyber-abbot crack the slightest of smiles. It felt odd to give back the handheld computer, which had kept him company ever since leaving Remota. But he was glad to be able to return the device, if it meant that Father Pius was alive to accept it.

'What can I do to help?' asked the cyber-abbot, whose eyes had now returned to normal.

Jake glanced out of the window at the Novu exploration ship. 'Nanoo is staying in this galaxy to help us, but he has his own ship. Father, can you take his place in our engine room?'

Father Pius nodded. 'I'm not a mechanic, but I know my way around a ship and I've studied engine technology.'

'When all this is over,' said Capio, 'I would like to hear more about your research, father. It sounds fascinating.'

The end of the Novu hangar deck split open like a ripe fruit to reveal the big black outside. Jake fired up the engine and squeezed the thrusters, but before the *Divine Wind* could move, the floor of the hangar deck rippled and the star frigate was spat out of the opening, shortly followed by the Novu exploration ship. A few seconds later, the giant Novu warships turned in unison and departed in a streak of light.

'Ahoy, *Divine Wind*,' said General Da Silva. 'Are you OK, my lord?'

'Yes, we're fine,' said Jake. 'We need another meeting, but first, there's something I have to do.'

Chapter 22

The Pirate King

'What is it?' asked Kella. 'What do you need to do?'

Jake reached for the package containing the crown of Altus. He pulled it out and held it up to the light.

'You should try it on,' suggested Kay.

'No,' said Jake, turning to Callidus. 'It's not mine.'

The fortune seeker shifted uncomfortably. 'I'm sorry, but placing a bit of metal on my head won't prove that I'm your father.'

'Well, I think it might.' Jake turned the crown over. 'Look at these sockets inside the rim. What if only the true ruler of Altus can wear this crown?'

Callidus peered at the mysterious holes and instinctively reached for the metal implants on his temples. He glanced at Jake, his eyes wide with wonder.

'What is it?' asked Capio. 'I don't understand.'

'Head-cuffs,' said Jake. 'What if Jorge Dasch was referring to Cal's metal studs? Perhaps they fit the sockets in this crown?'

'Head-cuffs?' Father Pius frowned. 'Those were banned centuries ago.'

'What are head-cuffs?' asked Kella.

'They're old technology,' explained the cyber-abbot, 'known on some worlds as secret keepers or memory binders. If someone has head-cuffs connected to their brain, they have to wear a retainer at least once a day, or else they would have their memories wiped.'

'Wear a what?' said Kay.

'A retainer,' repeated Father Pius. 'Special devices that were used to store memories. It was a very crude practice and the retainers often corrupted, leaving the user without their past.'

Callidus turned grey and backed away from the crown. He paced the bridge, his palms pressed over his metal studs. Jake followed his every step with anxious eyes.

'What does a retainer look like?' asked Kella.

'I've never seen one,' said Father Pius, 'but I expect that most of them were designed to be worn on the head, like a hat or a helmet.'

'Or a crown?' ventured Jake.

The cyber-abbot watched Callidus circle the bridge. 'Yes, why not.'

Jake examined the crown in his hands. It looked thick enough to conceal old-fashioned technology, but did it contain his father's lost memories?

'Why would anyone use such a device?' asked Kella.

'It was a good way to stop people talking,' said Father Pius. 'If someone was caught spying, their memories would be wiped before they could reveal anything.'

'It sounds exactly like the sort of thing the Protectorate would use to keep Altus a secret,' muttered Jake.

Callidus stopped pacing and stared at the gold crown, as though daring himself to touch its spikes. Jake held it out for the fortune seeker to take.

'Blast it!' Callidus marched over and seized the crown with shaking hands. He lifted it into the air and lowered it on to his dark wavy hair. There was a loud click as the metal studs slotted into place.

It was a perfect fit.

'Cal?' said Capio tentatively. 'Are you all right?'

Callidus dropped on to his knees and his face turned scarlet. He closed his eyes and cried out in pain.

'It's hurting him,' said Kella. 'We have to stop it.'

'No,' warned Father Pius. 'It could be dangerous to break the connection.'

Callidus hammered the metal floor with his fists as years of lost memories flooded his brain. Jake wanted to help, but what could he do? Now he understood why head-cuffs had been banned.

'I know who I am!' gasped Callidus.

Jake was barely able to talk. 'Who are you?'

Callidus opened his bloodshot eyes. He struggled to focus for a moment, before staring intently at Jake.

'I remember everything.'

Capio frowned at his friend. 'Cal?'

'No, not Cal. I am Andras Cutler, son of Jed and Kaya Cutler. Ruler of Altus and king of the pirates.'

Jake took a nervous step forward. 'You're my dad?'

Andras nodded and tried to stand, but his legs were too weak. Jake rushed forward and caught his father's arm to stop him falling.

'I found you, Jake,' said Andras. 'I kept my promise and followed you to Remota. I'm sorry it took so long.'

Jake could hardly believe what was happening. His heart swelled inside his chest and despite everything that was happening in the galaxy, a smile exploded on to his face.

'Is it you?' he asked. 'Is it really you?'

Andras laughed. 'It's me, I'm back.'

Jake, his father and the crew joined the remaining captains in the *Star Chaser* ballroom, as Jake had done

248

before the battle, only this time there were fewer people waiting for them. The once glamorous ball-room showed clear signs of combat damage, such as cracked plaster and shattered chandeliers. Most of the captains looked in a similar condition, with battle-weary faces and injured bodies.

As Jake entered, General Da Silva snapped shut his robot jaw and saluted. The other captains followed suit, each of them showing their respect in their own unique way, including Granny Leather-head, who blinked at him with her good eye. Rex Kent went to kneel, but stopped when he caught sight of Andras. It was the first time that Rex had seen Jake's father in eleven years and he was clearly lost for words.

'No speeches,' said Jake. 'Just a thank you. We lost some good people today, and robots, but their sacrifice was not in vain, because we saved the seventh solar system.'

'Thank the stars,' rejoiced Orana.

'The stars had nothing to do with it,' said Baden. 'None of us would be here today if it wasn't for Jake Cutler. He's the reason that our planets are safe.'

'Aye, but for how long?' grumped Granny Leatherhead. 'What will we do if those naval nitwits come back with reinforcements?'

Captain Harley narrowed her eyes. 'You're not suggesting that we wait here for them?'

'We might not have any choice,' said Jake. 'I want to go after Admiral Nex and take down the Interstellar Government as much as anyone, but we don't have enough ships left to fight our way to the first solar system.'

'I wouldn't be so sure, my lord.' It was hard to tell if General Da Silva was smiling, due to his robot jaw, but there was a definite twinkle in his eyes. 'Messenger ships from Reus, Vantos, Abbere and Torbana have arrived. They're sending us reinforcements: ten more warships, twenty more gunships and fifty more fighter craft.'

'And more will join us in the sixth solar system,' said Captain Swan. 'Father Benedict is already spreading the word about our victory. It seems that everyone wants to join the Independent Alliance, now that we've proven the Interstellar Navy can be defeated.'

Jake surveyed the heartened faces of the captains and he felt a rush of excitement. If there were reinforcements on their way, it meant that they still had a chance of reaching the capital planet, Domus, and taking down the Interstellar Government once and for all.

'Let's do it,' said Andras. 'We should attack now, while we have momentum and before the enemy recovers.'

General Da Silva eyed him curiously. 'And who are you?'

'Ignore him,' croaked Granny Leatherhead. 'He's just a fortune seeker.'

'Actually,' said Jake, 'he's my dad.'

There was a stunned silence while everyone stared at Jake and his father, until Granny Leatherhead burst into laughter.

'Nice one, Kid Cutler.'

'No, really,' insisted Jake. 'This is Andras Cutler, the rightful ruler of Altus. We discovered the truth less than an hour ago.'

'My lord,' said Rex, finding his voice and bowing his head. 'I recognised you instantly. Words cannot describe how good it is to see you alive after so many years.'

Granny Leatherhead stopped laughing. 'Well, bless my bloomers.'

'Indeed. It still feels strange to think of Altus as real.' General Da Silva pointed at Andras. 'Does this mean that he's in charge now?'

'No,' said Andras, stepping back. 'I may be the rightful ruler of Altus, but Jake is the leader of the Independent Alliance. He was the one who united the independent colonies, not me. It's his name that the Interstellar Navy fears.'

Captain Swan looked at Jake. 'What are your orders, my lord?'

Jake thought about this for a moment. 'I can't promise you another victory, but we do have a chance to stop the Interstellar Navy and overthrow the Interstellar Government. With reinforcements on their way, there will never be a better time to strike.'

Several of the captains nodded in agreement.

'What's our strategy?' asked Tark.

'No one has ever done anything like this before,' said Jake, unrolling a star chart that he had borrowed from the *Divine Wind*. 'But my dad is right, we should attack now while we have momentum. I want us to fight our way through the galaxy, one solar system at a time, gathering support and removing any naval vessels. When we reach the first solar system, we can seize control of Naval Command, before taking down the Interstellar Government.'

'Why don't we just cut through deep space to the first solar system?' asked Kay. 'It would be a lot easier.'

'I've thought about that,' said Jake. 'We'll have to face the remaining naval vessels at some point and I want to make sure the other independent colonies are safe. Besides, it's the Interstellar Navy who sneaks through deep space, not the Independent Alliance.'

General Da Silva nodded thoughtfully. 'In that case, we had better load up with supplies from the nearest colonies, because it's a long way to the first solar system.'

Jake glanced at the other captains. 'Are you with me?'

Captain Swan saluted. 'The *Star Chaser* is at your service, my lord.'

'So is the *Scarlet Sabre*,' said Captain Harley.

Captain Jia inclined her head. 'The *Shi Xianggu* awaits your command.'

'And you've got my single laser cannon,' said Baden. 'For what it's worth.'

'Mine too,' rasped Tark.

'Count me in,' said Orana.

Rex Kent smiled. 'Altus is with you.'

'My ship not have weapons,' said Nanoo, who had docked his Novu craft alongside the *Star Chaser*. 'But it have advanced scanners and strong shields. These useful to find enemy warships and protect innocent craft.'

Kay winked at Jake. 'I go where you go, shipmate.'

Jake looked expectantly at Granny Leatherhead. 'How about you?'

Granny Leatherhead rolled her single grey eye and cursed under her breath. 'Aye,' she said. 'And not because I'm a nice person, but because those naval warships got far too close to Reus for my liking. Crystals or no crystals, nobody threatens my family. It's time to put those mass-murdering maggots out of business for good.'

'It's agreed.' Jake rolled up the star chart. 'Let it be remembered that it was here, aboard this ship, that we came up with a plan to save the galaxy. We may not live to tell the tale, but every independent colonist will know our names.'

'In other words,' croaked Granny Leatherhead. 'Let's kick some naval butt.'

Chapter 23

Asteroid Field

Once the meeting was over, Jake walked back to the airlock with Granny Leatherhead, who was wearing her old combat spacesuit and clutching her silver skull-shaped helmet. There was something on Jake's mind, other than the mission ahead.

'Captain, can I ask you something?'

'You want to know why I'm called Granny Leatherhead, don't you? I'm surprised you haven't asked me before.'

'Actually, I was wondering if you saw a naval shuttle inside the Tego Nebula?'

'Oh,' she said. 'As a matter of fact, I did.'

'And did you destroy it?'

Granny Leatherhead shook her head. 'There was no point, it was already wrecked. I reckon it had been struck by lightning or its systems had overloaded with static. That nasty nebula claimed a couple of Altian ships as well.'

'It's a good job you didn't blow it up,' said Jake.

'Because it was carrying four mega-bombs.'

'What?' she screeched. 'Four mega-bombs? We could have been killed!'

'I know,' he said. 'It looks as though the Tego Nebula keeps finding ways to protect Altus.'

'No kidding.'

The two of them reached the airlock and stopped.

'Captain?'

'Yes, Jake.'

'Why do they call you Granny Leatherhead?'

'Honestly?' she croaked. 'I've had that nickname since I was a child, because I was born with thick leathery skin, like an old woman. It used to bother me, but not any more. Now I can't wait to hear my granddaughter call me Granny.'

'Have you ever met her?' he asked.

Granny Leatherhead's grey eye sparkled. 'No, but I expect that she's a gutsy little madam, like her mother.'

'You see, captain,' he said. 'There are things worth fighting for in this galaxy.'

Jake returned to the *Divine Wind* and waited for the fleet to finish its repairs. Within the hour, they were joined by more warships and a scattering of civilian craft. General Da Silva organised the vessels into battle formation and soon they were ready to depart. Jake observed the rows of multicoloured hulls on his display screen.

'United in our independence,' he whispered.

The speakers crackled.

'Ahoy, *Divine Wind*,' said General Da Silva. 'Are you ready, my lord?'

Jake took a deep breath and closed his eyes. It felt as though he was about to charge into a burning building or dive into a raging ocean.

'Ahoy, *Sol Dorado*,' he said, opening his eyes. 'Let's go and make some more history.'

Guided by Radio Interference and spurred on by their victory, the Independent Alliance left behind the captured naval vessels and proceeded to the sixth solar system. As predicted, more independent colony ships were waiting there.

'Check out those orange warships,' said Kay excitedly. 'There's at least six of them, plus a whole load of gunships and fighter craft.'

'Magnifty.' Jake's heart leapt. 'What are those small red and white ones?'

Kay squinted through the window. 'Medical craft. And that funny-looking rig is a mobile service port, which will come in useful for repairs.'

The arrival of each new vessel gave the crews a morale boost as the fleet edged towards the next battle.

Within a few hours, they reached Libertina, where the remains of the three Gork warships were already being stripped down by salvage crews. The alien wreckage served as a reminder that there were still more Gorks out there somewhere, waiting to fight them on the way to their first solar system.

But not in the sixth, which was suspiciously quiet. In fact, by the time the fleet reached Kella's home planet, Haven, Jake was starting to wonder if the Interstellar Navy had abandoned the solar system.

'Any sign of naval warships?' he asked, for what seemed like the hundredth time.

Kay shook her head. 'There's still nothing on the long-range scanner. We must have scared them off.'

'Perhaps,' said Jake doubtfully. 'It just seems so unlikely that they would leave two of their United Worlds unprotected.'

The fleet passed a small asteroid field on the other side of Haven. Jake cast his eyes over the jagged rocks. He doubted that he would ever be able to see one again without thinking of his father floating amongst them.

As he tried to block the image from his mind, a memory flashed before his eyes of a kalmar wrapped around the *ISS Colossus*. It had been the first time that Jake had seen a real space monster. The kalmar had appeared out of an asteroid field at the last moment and seized the super-destroyer, catching its crew by surprise. Jake shivered as he recalled the haunting sound of buckling metal around them.

The large asteroids made the perfect hiding place for something as big as a kalmar. That many rocks would confuse a scanner, leaving a passing ship blind until it was within striking distance. Any crew that wandered too close wouldn't stand a chance. Yes, they were the perfect hiding place. Perfect.

Jake jumped out of his seat. 'It's an ambush!'

His eyes combed the asteroid field for signs of movement, but it was too late. A squadron of concealed naval gunships were waiting with their weapons locked on to the Independent Alliance. The fleet had stumbled into a trap. Jake instinctively turned the *Divine Wind* away as laser bolts poured from the gaps between the rocks.

Before the rest of the fleet could rally, three small independent colony ships caught the brunt of the attack and they were ripped apart.

Nanoo quickly positioned his Novu vessel in front of the medical craft to protect them, while the *Sol Dorado* blasted the asteroid field with its broadside laser cannon. Andras and Capio opened fire, but most of their laser bolts hit the surrounding rocks.

'Ahoy, *Divine Wind*,' said General Da Silva. 'We're sitting ducks out here. Our gunners are struggling to hit the gunships and our fighters are reluctant to enter the asteroid field. What are your orders?'

'Do you have any torpedoes left?' asked Jake.

'A couple,' said the general. 'And the new ships might have some ... Wait, there's movement in the asteroid field. It looks as though the enemy is breaking cover. Are they charging at us?'

Jake checked his display screen. A dozen naval gunships were emerging from the asteroid field at speed.

'Why would they do that?' wondered Kay. 'There's no way that those idiots can defeat us in open space.'

As Jake watched, four red eyes glowed inside the shadows of the asteroids like burning coals, while giant green tentacles reached out to grab hold of the fleeing ships. There was something inside the asteroid field, something huge that made his blood run cold.

'It's a kalmar!' Jake activated the communicator. 'Attention, fleet. Destroy the gunships, but keep clear of the asteroid field.'

Jake guessed that the giant space monster had been drawn by the sound of fighting, much to the surprise of the naval crews. Its spaghetti-like tentacles wrapped around two of the gunships and pulled them back into the asteroid field, until both the kalmar and its prey disappeared from view.

'Whoa!' said Kay in awe. 'Can we keep it? We could call it Squidster.'

Jake ignored her and focused on the remaining naval gunships, which were now clear of the asteroid field. The communicator speakers crackled inside the bridge.

'Ahoy, independent colony fleet,' hailed one of the remaining naval gunships. 'Do not fire. This is Captain Larson or the *ISS Endeavour*. We surrender.'

'I'm not surprised,' laughed Kay. 'That kalmar must have given them a fright.'

'If it hadn't been for that kalmar, we would have lost a lot more vessels,' said Jake. 'From now on, I'm going to send scout ships ahead to check every single asteroid.'

Once the naval gunships were secured and their crews locked up, the Independent Alliance passed through the rest of the sixth solar system unchallenged. By the time the fleet left, its numbers had swelled to over thirty warships, forty gunships and a hundred fighter craft. Jake welcomed each new vessel personally, aware that every laser cannon increased their chance of success.

Father Pius joined Jake and Kay on the bridge as they greeted a brilliant-white warship from Ramost, which had several twin turrets positioned on top of stubby metal towers.

'This is going to get harder,' warned the cyber-abbot. 'There will be more and more United Worlds with each solar system, which means fewer and fewer reinforcements.'

'I know,' said Jake. 'But at least each battle will take us a step closer to the Interstellar Government and those wretchards in the Galactic Trade Corporation. How are you feeling now?'

'Honestly?' Father Pius attempted a smile, but it only lasted for a second. 'I'm not sure that I'll ever be the same again.'

'What happened to you on Remota?' asked Jake.

'I was taken prisoner. After you escaped, space pirates stormed the tech-library and killed the brothers, but they spared me. I was bundled into their assault craft and we left the planet. Before I could find out what they wanted, we met the *ISS Colossus* in orbit. I was taken aboard and placed in a prison cell, which is where I've been ever since.'

Jake groaned. 'But that means you were aboard the *ISS Colossus* when we were there. If only we had known, we could have saved you. Were you questioned?'

'Yes,' said the cyber-abbot gravely. 'Admiral Nex wanted to know what I had been researching and if it had anything to do with Altus. He asked about you, but what could I tell him? I had no way of knowing if you had made it off the planet.'

'Did he hurt you?'

'A little, but that was nothing compared with the black hole.'

Kay had been listening quietly, but she could no longer contain her curiosity. 'What's it like inside a black hole?'

'It's difficult to describe something that you cannot see,' said Father Pius. 'But I would say it was more like a planet than a hole. From what I could gather, a black hole is a spinning mass that rotates so fast, it attracts nearby objects and pins them to its surface, such as the *ISS Colossus*. The pull is so strong that not even light can escape, which is why black holes look so flat and featureless from the outside.'

'How did you get away?' asked Jake.

'I expect that most craft are destroyed on impact or their engines are too weak to break free, but the *ISS Colossus* is no ordinary ship. When we entered the black hole, its hull remained intact and the life support was operational. It took the crew months to find and repair the engine, working in complete darkness. The moment it was ready, the *ISS Colossus* blasted out of the black hole and returned to open space.'

'Which is when you found us?'

Father Pius nodded. 'It seems that fate is determined to bring us together.'

'No, not fate,' said Jake bitterly. 'Admiral Nex. He's the one who keeps interfering with our lives.'

There was a long way to go before the fleet reached the first solar system. Jake knew that the odds were stacked against them, but he was determined to think positively. However, his optimism was soon tested when they entered the fifth solar system.

Before they had even reached the first planet, the communicator speakers crackled to life.

'Ahoy, *Divine Wind*,' spoke the strangled voice of Tark. 'We've got incoming warships.'

Kay glanced at the long-range scanner and shook her head. 'Nothing.'

Jake flicked a switch on the communicator. 'Ahoy, *Half Moon*. I'm starting to think that you have a magic scanner.'

Tark rasped with laughter. 'Not magic. I'm picking up Gork communications.'

'Gork warships? How many?'

'At least ten and probably a few gunships.'

Jake cursed. He was sure that ten wasn't enough to defeat the Independent Alliance, but it could cause them serious problems.

'We knew that we would have to face the remaining Gorks sooner or later,' he sighed. 'It looks as though it will be sooner.'

'Not necessarily,' said Tark. 'Let me fly ahead and ask them to stand down. This is not their war, they are merely mercenaries, who have been promised their own planet in exchange for their services. It's possible that they will listen to me.'

Jake somehow doubted that the Gork warships would surrender without a fight, especially if the Interstellar Government had promised to give them something so important, but it was worth a try.

'OK,' he said. 'Go for it, Tark.'

'Thank you, my lord.'

The *Half Moon* tore ahead of the fleet and melted into the distance.

'He's a lot braver than most humans,' said Kay. 'It's funny, I would never have trusted a Gork, before I met Tark.'

Jake laughed. 'You're thinking of space pirates.'

An hour later, the Independent Alliance reached Zerost. Jake stared at the tiny white ice planet that had once been the home of the first spacejackers. Scargus had explained how the pirates had been peaceful colonists, until they were abandoned by their sponsor, the Galactic Trade Corporation. In desperation, the colonists had taken to the stars to steal supplies from passing ships. This had included Jake's ancestor, Captain Alyus Don, the first pirate king.

The communicator speakers interrupted his thoughts.

'Ahoy, *Divine Wind*,' said Nanoo. 'I picking up ship on my scanner. It coming fast.'

Chapter 24

Naval Command

The approaching craft appeared on Kay's long-range scanner and then the main display.

'It's the *Half Moon*.' Jake squinted at the screen. 'And it looks damaged.'

The converted racing ship had several new dents and a missing tailfin. Its hull was lined with blast marks and one section had completely peeled back like the skin of an apple.

'Ahoy, *Divine Wind*,' rasped Tark. 'I've located the Gork warships.'

'Ahoy, *Half Moon*,' said Jake. 'No kidding. Let me guess. They're not going to surrender?'

'No, they would rather die than accept defeat.'

Kay checked the scanner. 'Jake, we've got company. There are ten big blobs heading our way.'

Jake flipped a switch on the communicator. 'Attention, fleet. We're about to engage the remaining Gork crews. The enemy is tough and savage, but we outnumber them three to one. I know we can defeat them. Good luck, everyone.'

The Gork warships appeared on the main display. Jake scanned their bloated midnight blue hulls, which made them appear like a pod of robot whales. He knew from their previous encounter that the warships were well armoured, but the Gorks were easily fooled.

'Ahoy, *Divine Wind*,' said General Da Silva. 'All ships ready and awaiting your command.'

'Thanks, general.' Jake flipped a switch on the communicator. 'Attention, fleet. Fire torpedoes!'

Bursts of light erupted from the Independent Alliance as a hail of torpedoes launched into space. Jake watched the twenty missiles of various shapes and sizes hurtle towards the enemy, like some sort of mass rocket race.

'The Gorks are launching their own torpedoes,' reported Kay.

Jake had been expecting this.

'Attention, fleet,' he said into the communicator. 'I want you to divide our ships into two groups and leave a wide gap in the middle for the enemy torpedoes.'

The Gork pilots were not so quick to respond, and several of their warships took direct hits.

'Two down,' cheered Kay excitedly. 'Three more damaged, one of them badly.'

'Good,' said Jake. 'Because that was the last of our torpedoes and I expect the other ships are running low, until we can find somewhere to stop for supplies.'

The Independent Alliance attacked from both sides to confuse the enemy. Two of the Gork warships took evasive action and collided, smashing their hulls together. Independent Alliance warships, gunships and fighter craft fired with skill and ferocity. Jake was proud to see how much his fleet had improved. The crews were no longer clumsy and disorganised, but coordinated and battle-hardened.

Within minutes, three more Gork warships were reduced to stardust and the rest retreated.

'I don't believe it,' said Kay. 'Not a single one of our ships has been destroyed.'

Andras contacted the bridge. 'Well done, Jake. That was an incredible victory. Your mother always said that you were destined for great things. If only she could see you now.'

'Thanks, Dad.'

Jake had not meant to call him 'Dad', it had just slipped out, but it felt good to say it out loud.

'That's OK, son,' said Andras. 'Eleven years ago, I embarked on a mission to protect Altus. Now, we're going to finish the job together.'

Jake had waited a long time to be called 'son'. The word echoed in his ears and comforted him like a warm blanket. But there was no time to savour the feeling. They had a war to win.

The rest of the fifth solar system was mercifully quiet. A few naval gunships were on patrol near Gia, Gazear and Kalos, but they bolted at the sight of the Independent Alliance. When the fleet reached Ho Dan, it caught up with the last two Gork warships, which had run out of fuel cells. The Gorks were swiftly captured and locked in their own.

'Let's hope the next solar system is this easy,' said Jake.

A modest naval fleet met them in the fourth, which slowed the Independent Alliance down for a whole day and cost them several ships. This was the price they had to pay to liberate the independent colonies there, including Santanova, where the gathering had been held. In one particular skirmish, Captain Jia had strapped a stray asteroid to the front of the *Shi Xianggu* and used it as a battering ram to break the enemy defences. The unusual tactic had enabled the rest of the fleet to cross enemy lines and attack from behind.

Once the last battle had been won, the *Sol Dorado* chased the remaining naval craft out of the solar system. The rest of the Independent Alliance cleared any space mines, before stopping at Santanova for repairs and supplies. It was the first time that Jake and his crew had set foot on a planet since leaving Shan-Ti.

'We're halfway there,' said Kella encouragingly, as they breathed clean air and tasted fresh fruit. 'The Interstellar Government must know that we're coming by now.'

Jake glanced at Father Pius, who looked exhausted. His black robes were smeared with grease and engine oil. 'We can drop you at the monastery on Shan-Ti, if you want. I'm sure that Father Benedict would be pleased to see you.'

'No, thank you,' said the cyber-abbot. 'My place is aboard the *Divine Wind* with you, Jake. It's the most important ship in the galaxy right now and someone has to look after its engine.'

In the third solar system, the Independent Alliance pursued a collection of naval ships into the second, before forcing them to surrender on the edge of the first. The galaxy was now strewn with captured spacecraft and crumpled shipwrecks, which Baden had carefully mapped for later salvage. Jake had wondered a few times if there were any naval ships sneaking through deep space, but a passing crew of asteroid miners confirmed that nothing stirred beyond the seven solar systems, not even a kalmar.

There was only one place left to go.

'We're here,' whispered Kay, staring out of the window at the stars ahead. 'We actually made it.'

The Independent Alliance had reached the first solar system. Jake had never been to that part of the galaxy, but he had read about it on the stellar-net. The first was the only 'pure' solar system to be made up entirely of United Worlds. It was the location of the Interstellar Government, as well as Naval Command and the Galactic Trade Corporation.

Jake felt a shiver of anticipation as the *Divine Wind* crossed into the innocent-looking section of space. His fleet had fought its way across six solar systems and now the enemy had run out of places to hide. This would be where the war was won or lost.

It had taken the Independent Alliance weeks to reach the first solar system. Jake knew that the crews were exhausted and many of their ships were damaged. Most of the fleet had been patched up on Santanova, but some of the vessels were in such a bad way they were only held together with thin metal strips. Like most of the captains, Jake had only slept for a few hours between solar systems, but the end was so close now, he could taste it.

'Attention, fleet,' he said, rubbing his tired eyes. 'We're entering the last solar system under naval control. Whatever is left of the Interstellar Navy will be gathered here for a final stand. I doubt that they will go quietly, so I want everyone alert and ready to fight.'

According to Radio Interference, the remaining naval warships and gunships were joining together in a bid to protect the capital planet, Domus, including several special forces crews. These were supported by Galactic Trade Corporation vessels and a scattering of reserve troops.

'I'm afraid that we've not been able to locate Admiral Nex,' said Father Benedict. 'We've been trying to intercept communications from Naval Command for the last three hours, but they must have found a way to block us.'

Jake knew that the Independent Alliance's best hope would be to take out Naval Command first, before going after the Interstellar Government on Domus. That way, the remaining naval vessels would have to face the Independent Alliance on their own. If Admiral Nex was hiding anywhere, Jake reckoned it would be at Naval Command.

'How many stellar-net satellites does a planet need?' asked Kay, as the *Divine Wind* passed the United World of Ferres, which was surrounded by dozens of silver dishes. 'I'm surprised that anything can land there with all that space junk in the way.'

'It wouldn't surprise me if those things turned out to be space mines,' said Jake, picking up a flask of pirate tea that Kella had made him. 'The Interstellar Navy likes to play dirty.'

'How far is Naval Command?'

'Not far. It's positioned near the next planet, Borshet.'

Naval Command was a giant midnight blue space station, the size and shape of a small moon. It was the headquarters of the Interstellar Navy – the heart of the enemy. Most of its occupants were either senior officers or trainee cadets. Jake recalled seeing Naval Command for the first time on the *Interstellar News*. He had never seen anything so exciting and he had spent the next few days drawing it.

But those days were long gone. Now he was leading a mission to destroy the space station and hopefully its most senior officer, Admiral Nex. No more innocent ships or planets would be attacked. Naval Command had issued its last orders.

The fleet moved steadily forward, weapons at the ready. Kay watched her scanner expectantly, like an impatient angler.

'Where is everyone?' she muttered.

Jake had to admit that the lack of space traffic was creepy. It was like walking down a deserted street at night, and not how he had envisaged the mighty first solar system.

'It's the calm before the storm,' he said. 'We should enjoy it, while it lasts.'

The speakers crackled.

'Ahoy, *Divine Wind*. Nanoo speaking. I have Naval Command on scanner. It huge!'

'Ahoy ...' Jake hesitated. 'I can't believe that I'm only just asking this, but what is your ship called?'

Nanoo laughed. 'Novu craft not normally have names. This is exploration ship number eight. But I thinking of calling it *Cutler's Revenge*, after you.'

It was Jake's turn to laugh. 'In that case, ahoy, *Cutler's Revenge*. How many vessels are protecting Naval Command?'

'None,' said Nanoo. 'Not one blip on scanner.'

'What?' Jake had been expecting at least a dozen ships. 'It might be another trap. Keep on your guard and I'll warn the others to proceed with caution.'

The fleet slowly advanced on Naval Command and Jake had to admire the sheer scale of the space station. As they drew near, he could make out several neat rows of gun ports and a large United Worlds flag.

Kay whistled. 'That's one big bucket of blast-heads.'

'How long before we're in firing range?' asked Jake.

Kay checked her scanner. 'Any second now.'

Jake lunged for the communicator, but then stopped himself. 'Why isn't Naval Command preparing to defend itself?'

The space station sat innocently in front of them. Not a single gun port opened or fighter craft launched.

'It's empty,' said Kay. 'I'm not picking up any life signs in that sinister sphere.'

Jake had been convinced that Admiral Nex would have returned to this floating fortress.

'Yes, of course,' he whispered in astonishment. 'There's no Interstellar Navy left to command, other than the ships protecting Domus. Nex has abandoned his Naval Command. He must have taken the officers and cadets to join the remaining warships for a final stand.'

Kay smirked. 'Let's blow it up.'

'No,' said Jake, activating the communicator. 'Attention, all ships. Hold fire, Naval Command is empty. We need to save our laser bolts for the final battle. But take a good look at what we have achieved. This is a glimpse of our future galaxy, because once the war is over, there will be nothing left of the Interstellar Navy, except for shipwrecks and abandoned space stations.'

Jake turned off the communicator and paused to enjoy the moment. He had been itching to take revenge on Admiral Nex, but the old man would have to wait a bit longer. Naval Command had been defeated without a single shot being fired and there was only one more battle left to go. The end was in sight and it was time to finish the war.

With a final glance at the empty sphere, Jake steered the *Divine Wind* towards Domus.

Chapter 25

The Final Battle

For several hours, the Independent Alliance remained unchallenged as it advanced deeper and deeper into the first solar system, but that changed the moment the fleet passed the United World of Xavion.

'Naval vessels ahead,' reported Kay.

'How many?' asked Jake.

'Loads,' she said. 'It looks as though someone has sneezed on my scanner.'

'Well, we've not come here for a holiday. Do you think this old star frigate has one last battle left in her?'

Kay laughed. 'You had better believe it. The *Divine Wind* is like me. We might be a bit damaged and unpredicatable, but we're survivors.'

Jake checked the display screen. He could make out a blockade of vessels waiting beyond a small service port. There were naval warships and gunships, mixed together with special forces and Galactic Trade Corporation craft. He had not been expecting so many ships, but nothing was going to stop the Independent Alliance now.

'Attention, fleet,' he said. 'This is it, the last of the enemy. We've come so far together and we've lost many comrades along the way, but we must not hesitate. It ends here and it ends now. As your leader and a proud colonist, I ask of you one more time to roll out your laser cannon and attack!'

As though they were competing in a space race, every ship surged forward in a blur of colour. Jake squeezed the thrusters and the *Divine Wind* joined the charge.

'Battle stations,' he told the crew over the intercom. 'Good luck, everyone.'

The Independent Alliance released a tide of laser bolts as it drew level with the small service port.

Jake frowned at the display screen.

'What's wrong?' asked Kay.

'I don't like the look of that service port,' he said.

'Really?' Kay checked her scanner. 'It's completely deserted.'

'That's the problem. Why isn't the naval fleet using it? That service port is the perfect place to build defences or launch an ambush, but instead they're waiting for us beyond it, way beyond it, in open space ...' Jake wrenched the controls in the opposite direction and activated the communicator. 'Attention, all ships, pull back immediately, I repeat, pull –'

KABOOM!

A giant explosion tore apart the service port and swallowed half of the fleet. Jake shielded his eyes from the intense light and braced himself for the shockwaves. He had realised too late that the empty service port was a trap. The star frigate rocked violently as a shower of debris bombarded its hull.

'That was a guffing mega-bomb,' cried Kay, clinging to her scanner.

Jake waited until the ship steadied before reaching for the intercom.

'Is everyone OK?' he asked desperately. 'Hello? Is anyone there?'

'Aye,' said Andras from the gun deck. 'Capio is a bit bruised, but apart from that, we're OK.'

'I've cut my head,' moaned Father Pius from the engine room. 'From what I can see, the ship is functioning. However, our shields have been weakened by the blast.'

'I'm all right, but the medical bay is a mess,' said Kella. 'How's the rest of the fleet?'

Jake looked out of the window and was shocked to see a forest of mangled metal filling the spacescape.

'It's hard to tell how many survived,' said Kay. 'There's wreckage everywhere.'

'What about Nanoo and the Space Dogs?' asked Jake, fearing the worst.

Kay searched her scanner. '*Cutler's Revenge* and the *Dark Horse* were hit, but they were not destroyed.'

Jake cast his eyes over the lifeless wrecks and caught sight of a craft with black-and-white-chequered markings.

'Is that Orana's ship?' he asked, pointing.

'Aye, it looks as though she's alive, but her ship has lost power.'

Kay's gaze shifted and she gasped.

'What is it?' asked Jake.

'There's movement on the edge of the scanner,' she said. 'The enemy fleet is coming.'

Jake knew that they had only moments to act. He took one look at Orana's defenceless ship and instinctively steered the *Divine Wind* towards it. There was nothing he could do for those who had just died, but at least he could save one life.

However, before he could reach Orana, her cockpit separated from the rest of the craft and tumbled into space.

'Blast it, she's ejected.'

Jake went to follow, but the *Divine Wind* was blocked by a string of laser bolts.

'We've got incoming,' warned Kay. 'The enemy is approaching fast.'

Orana's cockpit drifted helplessly towards the enemy. Jake activated the intercom and gripped the controls.

'Father Pius, I want you to seal the inner hatch and lower the loading ramp. Cal ... I mean Dad, and Capio, we need some cover fire. Kella, get the medical bay ready.'

Kay raised her good eyebrow. 'You're going after her?'

Jake nodded. 'Too many people have died already. I'm not abandoning my friend.'

The *Divine Wind* snaked its way through laser bolts and wreckage, until it caught up with the tumbling cockpit. Jake could see Orana's terrified face peering through the misted glass.

'We're running out of time,' pressed Kay. 'We've got special forces incoming.'

'Just a little further.'

A laser bolt bounced off the front shield.

'Jake!'

'A few more seconds.' He carefully positioned the star frigate in front of the cockpit and slowed, until he heard it connect with the loading ramp and slide into the cargo hold.

'We've got her,' said Father Pius over the inter-com. 'From what I can see, she looks unharmed. I'm closing the ramp.'

BOOM!

BOOM!

Two laser bolts knocked the *Divine Wind* side-ways. Jake recovered and plunged the star frigate into a deep dive, closely pursued by at least three special forces ships. He used his best evasive moves, but the enemy stuck to the *Divine Wind* like heat-seeking torpedoes.

'I can't shake them,' he said.

More laser bolts peppered their weakened shields, narrowly missing the exhausts. Andras and Capio returned fire, but the special forces ships were not easy targets.

'Who can help us?' asked Kay.

Jake spotted the *Sol Dorado* and *Scarlet Sabre* up and running, but they were already fighting two naval warships. None of the other ships had stirred yet.

'We're on our own for now,' he said. 'But I've got an idea. Do you have any explosives on board from your spacejacking days?'

'There are a couple of old space mines and a crate of palm grenades in the cargo hold.' Kay gave him an inquisitive look.

'That will do.' Jake spoke into the intercom. 'Father Pius, I want you to wrap a string of palm grenades around every space mine you can find. When you're ready, get Orana to activate them and then dump the lot out of the airlock on my command.'

'I …' hesitated the cyber-abbot, who had only broken his vows of peace once to defend his monastery. 'Aye, Jake. You can count on us.'

'What are you up to, Kid Cutler?' asked Kay.

'It's something that I learnt from the Space Dogs,' he said. 'They used a similar tactic on the *ISS Colossus* during the battle of the black hole.'

BOOM!

The *Divine Wind* took another hit. A row of warning lights flashed across the control panel. The shields were starting to fail.

'Those special forces gunners know how to shoot,' said Kay appreciatively.

Jake sent the *Divine Wind* rolling towards a cluster of wrecked ships. 'How are you getting on, father?'

'We've found the space mines and we're wrapping them in palm grenades,' said Father Pius. 'Is this going to work?'

'There's only one way to find out.' Jake aimed for a small gap between the wrecked ships. 'You've got thirty seconds.'

If Jake could corral the special forces ships into a tight space, it might increase the chances of them hitting a space mine.

'You should be called Crazy Jake Cutler,' said Kay.

As the *Divine Wind* raced towards the gap, laser bolts blasted the wrecked ships around it.

'Now!' cried Jake into the intercom. 'Dump them now!'

The star frigate soared through the gap and several packages tumbled out of the airlock. Jake checked the rear display just in time to see the first of the special forces ships collide with at least two of the space mines.

BOOM!

A huge explosion ripped apart the ship and sent the surrounding wreckage spiralling in every direction. The other pilots attempted to swerve, but they were too late.

BOOM!

BOOM!

It had worked. All three special forces ships had been eliminated.

'Yes!' cried Kay. 'Not so special now, eh?'

'Three down,' said Jake. 'But plenty more to go.'

The *Sol Dorado* and *Scarlet Sabre* were still battling naval warships. A short distance away, the *Rough Diamond III* and the *Star Chaser* had recovered enough to fight a cluster of Galactic Trade Corporation vessels. Nanoo was using his powerful shields to protect several damaged ships, while the crews made urgent repairs. Just below him, the *Dark Horse* took on two special forces ships, supported by Rex Kent and the remaining Altian craft.

'We're outnumbered,' said Kay. 'At least half of our ships have been seriously damaged or destroyed, including the *Shi Xianggu* and *Half Moon*. Captain Jia and Tark are dead.'

Jake clenched his fists. 'We have to keep fighting. A large chunk of the enemy fleet is made up of reserves and cadets. We can do this, Kay, we can take them.'

Footsteps approached the bridge door.

'Hi there, Jakester,' said a familiar voice. 'I mean, my lord.'

Jake turned. 'Welcome aboard, Orana.'

'Thanks for saving my life,' said the ex-security guard, holding on to the doorframe. 'I owe you, big time.'

'Buy me an apple after the war and we'll call it even, but right now, I could use another shipmate on the gun deck. Can you fire a laser cannon?'

'Aye, my lord,' she said. 'I won the sharpest shooter award in training.'

'Excellent. The two new weapons are taken, but there should still be a working pink laser cannon in one of the old gun ports.'

'Pink?'

'It's a long story.'

The battle raged for hours of non-stop laser bolts and explosions. Despite destroying more ships, the Independent Alliance remained outnumbered. Jake wondered if there would come a point when his fleet would have to surrender, or if the crews would keep fighting until the bitter end. As he thought this, a special forces torpedo hit the *Scarlet Sabre* and blew apart the Shan-Ti warship. Jake watched in dismay as fragments of red camouflaged wreckage sailed past his window. Captain Harley was dead.

The *Sol Dorado* pulled up alongside the *Divine Wind*. Its thick green hull was severely damaged and it had a naval fighter wedged inside its airlock.

'Ahoy, *Divine Wind*,' said General Da Silva. 'My ship is not going to last much longer. Our shields are fading fast and our laser cannon are overheating. It has been an honour to serve with you, but I reckon it's over for me and the crew.'

Jake knew that they would be lost without the general. 'Ahoy, *Sol Dorado*. Don't give up yet. We have to keep fighting.'

'Aye, my lord, until the end.'

The *Divine Wind* soared between two naval warships, so Andras, Capio and Orana could blast their shields. Jake was determined to win the war, but victory was slipping out of reach fast. How much more could the Independent Alliance take? Doubts festered in his mind and drained his confidence. Was the battle already lost? No, they had come too far to fail now. He had to keep fighting, whatever the cost.

But what about his friends? Was his burning hatred for the Interstellar Government worth their lives? If he surrendered now, would his crew be spared?

'We've got more United Worlds ships on the scanner,' reported Kay.

Jake's heart sank with despair. 'How many?'

'At least twenty, but … Wait!'

'What is it?'

Kay scrunched up her face. 'Either my robotic eye is playing tricks on me, or they're attacking the naval warships.'

Jake stared at the display screen and saw that she was right. What was going on?

The new ships were marked with the United Worlds flag, except it had been crossed out with red paint.

'Rebels!' he cried.

'What?'

Jake could barely contain his excitement. 'Before she was arrested, Kella's sister, Jeyne, was helping a group of United Worlds citizens to rebel against the Interstellar Government. It has to be them, the rebels!'

To their delight, the rebel craft swarmed over the naval warships and quickly turned the tide of battle.

'Fire, you dogs!' croaked Granny Leatherhead, over the communicator. 'We've got those naval nasties on the run. Fire!'

The Independent Alliance pushed forward with everything it had left. A final wave of laser bolts and torpedoes mixed with the shots from the rebel ships to bombard the enemy vessels. Jake watched the naval defences crumbled like snow in the rain. When the last of the warships imploded, the remaining gunships and fighters fled, leaving only a few cadet ships to be rounded up.

'We've done it,' cheered Kay. 'We've won the war!'

Jake stared in disbelief at the clouds of debris scattered around Domus. He shuddered to think how many people had lost their lives.

If it hadn't been for the rebels …

If they hadn't shown up when they did …

If the Interstellar Navy had been victorious …

Jake couldn't bare to think about it, but it would have been a very different ending.

An eerie silence now replaced the thunder of laser cannon. Jake had become accustomed to the roar of battle and he half expected to hear something explode. Was it over? Was the galactic war really finally over?

'Not yet,' he said. 'It's not over until we take down the Interstellar Government.'

Chapter 26

The Interstellar Government

Jake stood with his father on the bridge of the *Divine Wind*, as it descended on the capital planet, Domus. The battered star frigate was accompanied by *Cutler's Revenge*, the *Dark Horse*, the *Sol Dorado*, the *Star Chaser*, the *Rough Diamond III*, a handful of Altian craft and a squadron of rebel ships.

Orana had offered to pilot the *Divine Wind*, so Jake could spend time with Andras. Capio remained on the gun deck, Kella prepared the medical bay and Father Pius kept the engine working. There was no longer any need to watch the scanner, because the enemy fleet had been defeated, so Kay passed the time by shooting bubbles at the window.

The Independent Alliance entered the planet's atmosphere and landed on the surface unchallenged. Jake and the other pilots set down the ships on the lawns outside the largest government building in the galaxy. A crowd of nervous citizens watched as angry colonists and rebels poured out of the airlocks, before passing a row of naval hover-bikes and gathering by a set of huge concrete steps.

Jake paused in front of the imperious building, which towered defiantly before them. This was it, the end of their journey. Inside the blue marble walls cowered the Interstellar Government. He brushed back his thick brown hair and flattened his crumpled Altian uniform.

'What are we waiting for?' asked General Da Silva. 'Victory awaits!'

Jake unsheathed his golden cutlass and led the charge up the sweeping steps to a pair of great glass entrance doors. There were no security barriers or guards outside. Was the Interstellar Government arrogant enough to think that no one would dare to attack them? Had they believed that the Interstellar Navy would always be around to protect Domus?

As Jake reached the top, his eyes caught a flicker of light. A plasma bolt smashed through the glass doors and hit him square in the chest. With a stab of pain, he was knocked clean off his feet and on to the hard concrete surface, while shards of glass rained down around him.

'Jake!' cried Andras, crouching by his side.

'I'm OK,' coughed Jake, pulling his smoking shirt open to reveal his laserproof vest. 'I'm just winded.'

Inside the building stood a group of armed guards, their plasma rifles at the ready. Jake could make out their nervous expressions, as they prepared to defend the entrance hall from the angry horde.

'Attack!' barked General Da Silva.

A wave of people rushed the doors and the sound of lasers mixed with the plasma fire. Jake rolled out of the way as two injured rebels fell backwards, clutching their wounds. He clambered to his feet, holding his own throbbing chest, while his sword hung by his side.

'Keep low,' said Andras. 'Until you catch your breath.'

Jake was about to argue when someone shouted 'Palm grenade!' and everyone ducked for cover. He threw himself to the floor as the device detonated inside the building.

BOOM!

There was an enormous bang and a burst of smoke poured from the doorway. A few surviving guards staggered outside, their uniforms bloodied and their hands in the air.

Jake waited for the smoke to clear and the guards to be taken prisoner, before raising his cutlass. 'Now let's go and see their masters.'

There was a roar of approval and several more swords thrust into the air. Jake stormed the government building flanked by his father, his friends and his comrades. Their gravity boots pounded the tiled floor like a cascade of drums, as they swept through the long corridors.

'Gather them up,' ordered Jake. 'Gather them all up and place them under arrest.'

The Independent Alliance and the United Worlds rebels emptied the meeting rooms, while Jake and his shipmates followed signs for the parliament chamber. Any workers they came across screamed and barricaded themselves in their offices, except for one burly official who came at them with a chair, but Kodan took him down with a single punch.

'There is it,' said Nanoo, pointing to a huge archway at the end of the passage. 'Parliament chamber.'

Two troopers stood defiantly in front of the entrance doors, wearing ceremonial silver helmets and breastplates over midnight blue tunics. As far as Jake could tell, they did not carry plasma rifles or palm grenades. But their forked spears looked sharp enough to skewer a person.

'Halt!' shouted one of the troopers, his spear shaking.

'It's over,' said Jake, firmly. 'The Interstellar Navy has been defeated and you're outnumbered. There's no need for you to die here today.'

The two guards glanced nervously at each other, but held their positions.

'Let me shoot them,' hissed Granny Leatherhead.

Jake shook his head. There had been enough blood spilt in space.

'This is your last chance,' he warned them. 'If you put down your weapons and surrender, I give you my word that you will not be harmed.'

Before the men could respond, a mechanical roar and a gust of wind flooded the corridor. Jake twisted around to find the source of the commotion. The others scurried out of the way, as something large and midnight blue approached them at speed.

'Ahoy-hoy!' cried a familiar husky voice.

'Kay?' said Jake.

A naval hover-bike tore along the corridor, its engine revving and its headlights on full beam. Kay sat perched on its back, ducking the low-hanging lights as she accelerated towards the chamber doors. Jake threw himself to the side a second before the hover-bike reached him.

'Catch me!' cried Kay, leaping from the saddle.

Jake dropped his cutlass and caught Kay in his arms, before the pair of them crashed to the floor.

'I thought you didn't know how to ride those things,' he said.

Kay grinned. 'There's a first time for everything.'

The hover-bike careered towards the startled troopers, who abandoned their spears and dived to the floor.

CRASH!

It hit the entrance doors with such force, they smashed open, and the whole corridor shook. Jake climbed to his feet, snatched up his cutlass and ran towards the opening. He leapt over the crumpled hover-bike and into the parliament chamber, where he was greeted by gasps and shrieks of terror. At last, he had reached the Interstellar Government.

Hundreds of sour-faced politicians sat in rows around the chamber, which looked like the inside of a giant pumpkin, apart from its pale blue walls and glass dome roof. Jake noticed that many of the people wore the diamond brooches of the Galactic Trade Corporation. A few of them stood up, but there was nowhere for them to go, they were trapped and they knew it. The chamber had been their last sanctuary.

Andras entered and fired his laser pistol at the floor. The room fell instantly silent, except for the entrance doors swinging on their broken hinges.

Jake walked into the centre of the chamber and glared at his enemy. The Interstellar Government had once been honest and peaceful, set up to serve the United Worlds. But over the centuries, it had been corrupted by greed. Now the politicians used their power to attack innocent worlds. Jake felt sick to think that these people had started a galactic war, so the Galactic Trade Corporation could mine more of the independent colonies for crystals.

'Your attempts to take over the galaxy have failed.' His words echoed in the huge chamber. 'I am Jake Cutler, leader of the Independent Alliance. My fleet has fought its way across the seven solar systems and many lives have been lost, but that ends today. No more Interstellar Navy. No more Galactic Trade Corporation. No more Interstellar Government. The war is over and you're all under arrest –'

'Over my dead body,' snarled a scratchy voice.

A lone figure in an extravagant mauve uniform stepped out of the crowd and unsheathed a long sabre. His polished gravity boots squeaked with each step and his rows of medals rattled like windchimes. The man stopped in front of Jake and narrowed his cold, venomous eyes.

'Admiral Nex,' said Jake, through gritted teeth. 'I wondered where you were hiding.'

'What have you done?' hissed the admiral. 'Who will protect the seven solar systems now?'

'Protect?' said Jake angrily. 'Is that what you call murdering innocent people for crystals?'

Admiral Nex glared at him. 'What do you know about crystals, boy? You were too young to remember the last shortage. If you think war is bad, wait until disease and famine grip this galaxy. What do you know about anything?'

'He knows enough,' said Andras, moving next to Jake.

'Captain Stone,' sneered Admiral Nex. 'So you're still hanging out with spacejackers, eh?'

'Actually, my name is Cutler. Andras Cutler.'

The sneer wiped from the admiral's face. His eyes darted between Jake and his father, perhaps searching for common features. He nodded slowly and grimaced.

'You'll always be Stone to me,' he said, his sword hand pulling back. 'Stone dead.'

Admiral Nex lunged at Andras with his sabre. He was faster than he looked and Andras had no time to react, but Jake had anticipated what was about to happen. With lightning speed, he raised his cutlass to block the blow. The blades clashed in a golden blur and Admiral Nex was forced backwards. He scowled at Jake and changed his footing.

'I was naval fencing champion seven times,' he said arrogantly. 'Do you think you can take me, boy?'

Andras started to protest, but Jake was not afraid. With a confident smile, he raised his cutlass. 'Let's find out.'

Admiral Nex attacked, thrusting his sword with deadly precision. Jake ignored his bruised chest and fought back, fending off each blow. Nex cursed and lashed out with a series of random strikes, which Jake managed to deflect.

'Die, you little wretchard,' raged the admiral.

'You first,' said Jake, who was using every trick that Scargus had taught him.

Andras, Capio, Kella, Nanoo, Kay and the Space Dogs stood in a tight semi-circle behind him, their weapons raised.

'Come on, Kid Cutler,' croaked Granny Leather-head. 'You can take him.'

Jake blocked two more blows and jumped a low swipe, but he landed badly and lost his balance. Admiral Nex took advantage and slashed Jake with his sabre, cutting his face and scratching his eye implant. Jake howled with pain and recoiled, blood pouring from the wound. His damaged eye implant flickered and he struggled to focus.

'Any last words?' asked Admiral Nex, raising his sabre.

Jake forced himself to concentrate on the fight. With one eye closed, he glared at Admiral Nex and said the only words that came to mind.

'Kiss my cutlass.'

With a bloodcurdling cry of rage, Admiral Nex brought down his sword. Jake reached up, trapped the sabre blade under his arm and twisted on the spot, wrenching the sword out of his enemy's hand. Admiral Nex stumbled forward and fell to the ground. Jake cast the sabre to the side and raised his golden cutlass over his head.

There were so many reasons why he despised Admiral Nex: the monastery attack on Remota, Amicus Kent, Vigor-8, his eye implants and eleven years without his father. No one would blame Jake for killing the cruel admiral – he would probably be regarded as a hero for doing it – but something held him back. As he stood over the cowering man, he realised that there was no need. He had already won. Admiral Nex was finished.

'Algor Nex, I'm arresting you for galactic war crimes and for destroying a defenceless Altian ship eleven years ago,' he said calmly, lowering his cutlass and mopping his bloodied face with his sleeve.

'It's the end of the seven solar systems,' mumbled the admiral feverishly. 'The crystal shortage will finish us. I was supposed to find Altus. You were supposed to help me.'

Jake shrugged. 'Never trust a space pirate.'

Andras placed a hand on his shoulder. 'Are you all right, son?'

Jake turned and smiled. 'Agonisingly happy.'

'That cut looks nasty,' said Andras. 'We'd better get Kella to take a look –'

'Watch out!' warned Kay.

Jake turned to discover Admiral Nex pulling a combat knife from his boot. His eyes were wild and his face was deranged.

'You've destroyed the galaxy,' roared the admiral, hurling himself at Jake.

'No!' cried Andras.

Jake closed his eyes and waited for the knife to pierce his skin. There was a loud noise and something crashed to the floor. He opened his eyes to discover Admiral Nex slumped at his feet, dead. Granny Leatherhead stood nearby, her chunky laser pistol aimed at the spot where Admiral Nex had been moments ago.

'Nobody messes with the Space Dogs,' she croaked, lowering her pistol.

Jake looked upon the broken body of Admiral Nex and he felt no pity. His greatest enemy was gone. At last, he and his father could lay the ghosts of their past to rest.

Chapter 27

The Galactic Senate

Within hours of disbanding the Interstellar Government, Jake sent envoys to every planet in the seven solar systems, including independent colonies and United Worlds. His message was simple: *The galactic war is over and together we will build a better galaxy.* Kella volunteered to deliver these words to Ur-Hal, the maximum security prison planet, along with orders to release her sister, Jeyne.

The next morning, the stellar-net was restored and the following day several *Interstellar News* crews arrived on Domus, requesting interviews with the 'freedom fighter' Jake Cutler.

'What do I tell them?' Jake asked his father.

'You'll think of something,' said Andras. 'Come on, son, the galaxy is waiting.'

In the busy week that followed, Jake worked with delegates from the different planets to set up a new galactic senate, where everyone would have an equal voice. There would no longer be independent colonies or United Worlds, but fifty-six separate planets working together, including Altus. Jake proposed that the senate chambers be located somewhere central, such as Santanova, on the site where Lugar city had been destroyed, so the galaxy would always remember those who had lost their lives.

Several of the delegates suggested that Jake be the first chair of the galactic senate, but he refused.

'I may have led the Independent Alliance to victory,' he said. 'But I still have a lot to learn about politics. Besides, I've got some catching up to do with my dad and we have a planet to bring out of hiding. Therefore, I nominate Kristina Lemark from Shan-Ti.'

Kristina had only arrived on Domus that morning and she was still suffering from space lag after her long journey. The nomination for chair person caught her by surprise, but it proved popular with the other delegates.

'This is an unexpected honour,' she said, at a ceremonial feast that evening. 'How can I refuse such an incredible opportunity to help shape the future of our galaxy?'

The first galactic senate meeting was held the following week in a temporary location on Santanova, in the fourth solar system. Within the first few minutes, the planetary leaders voted to break up the Galactic Trade Corporation and arrest its directors for corruption.

'What are we going to do about the crystal shortage?' asked the new president of Domus.

'I can help to solve that problem,' said Andras, who was dressed in a smart maroon uniform, complete with the crown, the sword and the pendant of Altus. 'I'm going to set up a small crystal mining operation on my planet. If we drill each of the moons in moderation, there should be enough crystals to avoid a mega-depression.'

'What about crystal hunters and space pirates?' asked the president of Reus. 'Who will protect our planets and ships?'

It was agreed that the profits from the Galactic Trade Corporation would be used to fund a new fleet of warships to keep peace in the galaxy, under the command of General Da Silva. Instead of a single Interstellar Navy, the new fleet would take crews from each of the fifty-six planets.

Kella joined them on Santanova, where she introduced everyone to her sister, who had needed healing before she could travel. Jeyne was tall and skinny with hazel brown eyes and long blonde hair. Her skin was pale and gaunt from her time on Ur-Hal.

'Thank you, Jake,' said Jeyne, shaking with emotion. 'Kel has told me everything that you've done for us. How can we ever repay you?'

Jake smiled. 'You can start by accepting a job.'

'A what?' Jeyne looked confused.

'We need someone trustworthy to run the new cystal mining operation on Altus,' explained Andras. 'It might be a bit bigger than your old family crystal mine, but you can always bring your parents to help, if you want. What do you reckon?'

Jeyne glanced at Kella for guidance, who nodded encouragingly.

'OK, yes,' she said impulsively. 'I'll do it.'

'What about you, Kella?' asked Jake. 'Are you going to help your big sister?'

Kella grinned. 'Actually, I was thinking of starting a crystal healing school and where better than Altus?'

'That great idea,' said Nanoo. 'Maybe you teach me?'

'Does that mean you're coming too?' asked Jake.

Nanoo nodded. 'Yes, there are many planets to see and cultures to study, before I return to Taan-Centaur. I thinking that Altus is good place to start my observations.'

Jake laughed and embraced his two friends. Words could not describe how much they meant to him. And after everything they had been through together, he knew that they felt the same.

'Proud to be space pirate kin?' he asked them.

'Aye,' they replied. 'Space Dogs forever!'

When it was finally time to return to Altus, Jake and the others were offered passage by Captain Swan, who was himself keen to return to the seventh solar system to see his family on Reus. Rex Kent insisted on escorting the *Star Chaser* along with the remaining Altian craft. On the day of departure, thousands of people came to Santanova to wave them off, including their friends and comrades, who lined up in front of the battle-scarred pleasure cruiser to say goodbye.

General Da Silva was first in the queue. He stood to attention and saluted.

'Thank you, my lord,' he said, his polished robot jaw gleaming in the sunlight. 'It really has been an honour to serve with you.'

Jake returned the salute with the upmost respect. 'It should be me thanking you, general. The Independent Alliance would have been lost without you and the *Sol Dorado*. Take care of the galaxy. It's under your protection now.'

'Are you sure that we cannot convince you to stay?'

'I'm afraid not,' said Jake. 'But don't worry, we'll come and visit soon, now that Altus is coming out of hiding.'

Next in line was Baden Scott, who had shaved especially for the occasion. 'I'll see you around, kiddo. My crew is heading out tomorrow. We're going to take the *Rough Diamond III* to clear up those naval wrecks. That should keep us busy for a while.'

'All the best, Baden.' Jake lowered his voice, so only the salvage captain could hear him. 'Let me know if you ever fancy removing a naval shuttle from a nebula cloud.'

'Aye, why not, that sounds like a worthy challenge.'

Father Pius was wearing his black robes of order and clutching his handheld computer, which still looked as though it had been trampled on by a herd of house robots.

'Goodbye, Jake,' said the cyber-abbot. 'I'm so very proud of you. When Amicus Kent left you at the monastery on Remota, he told me that you were special. I never doubted it for a second.'

'Thanks, father. I don't know where I would be today, if you hadn't taken me in that night.'

Kella peered over Jake's shoulder. 'Is it true that you turned down a promotion to become a cardinal, father?'

Father Pius smiled modestly. 'It was a flattering offer, but I'm going to return to Remota, so I can rebuild the monastery on Temple Hill.'

'And I've offered to help him,' said Capio, excitedly. 'Father Pius thinks that I would make a good novice.'

Andras shook hands with the two men. 'Thank you, both of you, for everything that you've done for us. We owe you so much, more than crystals could ever repay. But rest assured, you will have enough money to build the best monastery in the seven solar systems.'

Nanoo handed Father Pius a data crystal. 'This contain information about Taan-Centaur and Novu technology. I thinking you find it interesting.'

'We'll come and visit you soon,' promised Jake. 'Just make sure the new monastery has a good banister for sliding down.'

'I'll keep an eye on them, Jakester,' said Orana. 'The word on the stars is that Remota still needs a new mayor and I'm thinking of applying for the job.'

Jake smiled. 'I'd vote for you. Let me know if you ever need anything from Altus. After all, Remota is our closest neighbour.'

Orana pulled a fresh apple out of her pocket and tossed it to him. 'Here, I owe you this for saving my life.'

Jake caught the apple and grinned. 'Thanks.'

The Space Dogs were next to say goodbye. Granny Leatherhead presented each of them with an embroidered patch to commemorate the first ever galactic war.

'What will you do now?' asked Jake.

'We're quitting spacejacking,' said Farid, proudly. 'It no longer feels right without Galactic Trade Corporation ships to plunder, so we're going to start a legitimate cargo hauling company instead. That is, everyone except the captain.'

Jake looked curiously at Granny Leatherhead.

'I'm going to find my daughter and granddaughter on Reus,' she croaked. 'It's about time that I turned respectable and behaved like a proper grandparent, before I miss any more of their lives.'

'Good for you,' said Jake. 'I bet they will be proud to have a war hero as their granny.'

Andras unsheathed the sword of Altus and offered it to Granny Leatherhead. 'Here, I know that Jake promised to give you this golden cutlass, if you helped him to save the independent colonies. A deal is a deal.'

Granny Leatherhead stared at the sword for a moment, before pushing it away with her finger.

'Keep it,' she said. 'It belongs to you and your planet. I've got plenty of crystals for my retirement, thanks to Rex Kent. He sorted us out with the crates we were owed, plus a few more for our trouble.'

Jake hugged her. 'Thank you for doing the right thing when it counted, captain.'

Granny Leatherhead cracked a smile. 'You take care of yourself, Kid Cutler.'

Kay was the last person to bid them farewell. The teenage space pirate held out a feather duster and winked at Jake with her good eye. 'A little something to remember me, shipmate.'

'Ha!' laughed Jake. 'Don't worry, I won't be forgetting you any time soon. Are you sure that you won't come with us to Altus?'

'Nah,' she said, scrunching up her nose. 'It's nice of you to offer, but that Tego Nebula plays havoc with my robotic eye. I'm going to sell what's left of the *Divine Wind* and join the Space Dogs. It sounds as though they have a vacancy.'

There was an awkward silence and Jake found himself unable to move. It was strange to say goodbye after they had spent so much time together. Kay had been by Jake's side throughout the entire war. This meant that she was more than a friend to him, she was his sister-in-arms.

'I'm going to miss you,' he said. 'We made a good team.'

Kay beamed. 'The best.'

Without warning, she launched herself on to Jake and squeezed him tightly.

'Keep an eye on the stars, Crazy Kay Jagger,' he said, patting her back.

Kay let him go. 'And stay out of trouble, Kid Cutler.'

Kella, Nanoo and Jeyne boarded the *Star Chaser*, but Jake and Andras paused on the ramp to take one last look at the friends they were leaving behind. Jake knew that they would all stay in touch. After everything they had been through, their bond was strong enough to last a lifetime, no matter how much time passed or how far they travelled. Besides, it wasn't such a big galaxy.

'Goodbye, shipmates,' he muttered.

'Come on, son,' said Andras. 'Let's go and make some memories.'

The two of them boarded the *Star Chaser*, which was preparing to take off. In the guest quarters, Jake strapped himself into a comfortable bed and braced himself for launch. As he lay there, listening to the engine, he felt a wave of exhaustion wash over him. It had been an incredible few months and they were lucky to be alive. The galaxy was now safe and they could finally rest. He glanced across the room at his father lying on the opposite bed. To his people, Andras Cutler was the true ruler of Altus and the pirate king. Jake was just pleased to have his dad back. He smiled and closed his eyes.

Any second now, the crew would turn the engine to full throttle and release the thrusters. Any second now, the *Star Chaser* would rise up into the sky. Any second now, they would head into outer space and set course for the Tego Nebula.

After eleven years, Jake and his father were heading home, together.

Huw Powell was born in August 1976 in Bristol, England, during the hottest summer on record. He grew up in the village of Pill in North Somerset, where he wrote his first stories for friends and family. His best subjects at school were English Literature and Art, which he went on to study at university. Huw started writing novels while working in London for Lloyds Bank. He now lives in Portishead with his wife Beata and their two energetic sons. When he's not sat at his computer, Huw enjoys watching films and spending time with his family.